WANT TO BE KEPT UP TO DATE WITH AGATHA FROST RELEASES? ***SIGN UP THE FREE NEWSLETTER!***

www.AgathaFrost.com

You can also follow **Agatha Frost** across social media. Search 'Agatha Frost' on:

Facebook
Twitter
Goodreads
Instagram

ALSO BY AGATHA FROST

Other

CHAPTER ONE

*U*nwilling to let the incline of Park Lane break her, Claire Harris forged up the sludgy road with her shopping trolley packed to the brim with candles. The scarf Damon had haphazardly thrown about her in her rush out of the shop wasn't doing a great job of keeping her neck warm, but it was perfectly funnelling her short, sharp breaths to steam up her specs.

She peered over her frames. The side entrance of the park was only a stone's throw away. A haze of fog swallowed up the rest of the lane before the road curved out of sight, multicoloured Christmas lights flashing somewhere in the distant vapour. Behind the rows of trees and the wall separating the park and the street, the sun – nothing more than a silver disc – fought through the bare branches in challenging angelic stripes. The blend of the sun and fog gave the biting winter morning a dreamlike quality though that could be Claire's steamed glasses.

Wrapping her gloved fingers tighter around the trolley handle, Claire pushed through the point of the hill where the steepness usually threatened to topple her backwards. Just when she felt her legs begin to buckle, the high stone wall curved away to Starfall Park's side entrance. She squeezed the trolley through the bollards and paused to catch her breath, glad of the flat surface.

A lifetime of living in Northash, a village consisting entirely of hills, didn't make them any easier. Still, looking down at the glass finish of the curved path in the park, Claire knew she'd taken the easy route. The front gates were a tourist thing – a quirk of the locals – though Claire dared anyone to attempt the climb today. With the craft fair she was on her way to due to start in an hour, she was surprised somebody hadn't been out to grit the paths yet.

Shapes moved about in the mist. Dog walkers, no doubt, but the only person within earshot was a man perched in a squat by the marble fountain between Claire and her destination, Starfall House. He had a camera aimed at the fountain, now merely decoration from a bygone time.

Approaching headlights from the bottom of Park Lane forced Claire from lingering any longer at the side entrance. Claire pushed the trolley onto the ice as the car wheels sprayed slush onto the backs of her socks poking out of her trainers. The grit stuck to her shoes fought against the slippery surface, but the ice was as smooth as freshly polished silverware.

As careful as Claire tried to make her steps, the trolley tugged her forward, having different ideas. The path across to the house, which she'd assumed was directly opposite the side entrance, sloped on a diagonal decline. She locked her knees, and the trolley pulled.

"You might want to watch out," Claire called as she and the clattering candles slid toward the man and the marble fountain at an alarming speed. "I don't think I'm in control of this in the slightest!"

The flash of a robin's red breast fluttered away from the fountain as the man spun around, and for a moment, she felt a surge of guilt at having ruined his peaceful morning. He flashed the camera in her direction, blinding her in an instant.

Free falling along the ice, hauled by the weight of her lovingly handmade creations, Claire wondered if she'd wheel back down the hill all the way. Suppose she crashed into the clock tower in the square. She'd give Damon more to think about than trying to guess the flavour of The Hesketh Arms' annual 'Mystery Crispmas' competition.

Conspired against by her candles and ice.

Quite a way to go.

"Are any of us?" a soft, smooth voice asked.

Claire realised she wasn't just blinded by the flash; she was clenching her eyes shut. She relaxed them. The birdwatcher had a hand and a foot stretched out, slowing the trolley to a halt by the fountain. Claire's feet gave a wobble as she skidded toward him, and he caught her. She grabbed the marble sink edge and let out a disbelieving laugh, charged with adrenalin. She'd resigned herself to her fate far too quickly.

"And that's why I don't go ice skating," Claire announced, dragging her chin, moistened by her panicked breathing, over the top of the scarf. Suddenly, it was too itchy, and she ignored the urge to yank it away, not that she had a free hand. "Are any of us what?"

"In control," he said, lips framed by a fair beard silvering at the edges, below rosy cheeks as round as fresh apples. "Quite the thing to exclaim as you're hurtling to your doom."

From his accent alone, he wasn't local. His refined vowels placed him from somewhere southern enough that Claire must have sounded like a Northern extra from a teatime soap to him. Still smiling, he peered into the trolley and scanned the many candles. His crystal blue eyes were wide and expressive under the shade of his hat, a flat cap that would have looked more natural upon the head of a man closer to Claire's father's age. She guessed the birdwatcher who'd saved her from almost certain death was somewhere in his mid-to-late thirties, like her.

"That picture I snapped might come in handy to show the police," he said, his tone taking on a serious edge. "This many candles, I can only assume you're on the run?"

"There was a sale on," she said flatly. "I smell a candle, it has to go in my trolley. I simply couldn't help myself." He arched a brow, cocking his head back at her. "They're from my shop," she admitted. "I was on my way to Starfall House for the craft fair, but now I'm not sure I want to move from here until someone comes and grits us a path to safety."

"Then that must make you Claire." He stretched out a leather-gloved hand, and she offered him her wool-wrapped digits. He gave a lingering handshake, his eye contact firm. "I'm Mark. And your mother knows you far too well. She sent me out here to see if you'd slipped." He chuckled. "You were ten minutes late five minutes ago, and she's quite the clock watcher."

Janet, her mother, had only called to tell her about a stall becoming available twenty minutes ago. Claire had been in the middle of her first coffee, still preparing the shop with Damon for the Friday ahead. She took a calming breath – Mark didn't seem too scarred from his interaction with Janet Harris. "You know my mother?"

5

"Not in the slightest, but she doesn't seem like a woman who'd have taken 'no' as an answer."

"Sounds to me like you *do* know her." Claire looked to the house, and as though she knew she was being spoken about, Janet appeared in the Victorian conservatory jutting off the kitchen. "For all her faults, she got me into this fair, as last minute as it is."

"*Claire!*" Janet cried, waving an arm from the back door. "I see you've met Mark." Hugging herself against the cold, she looked around the empty park. "You'll have to go around to the front, Claire. You'll never get that thing up these stairs. And what are you doing clinging onto that fountain, and where did you get a trolley?"

"Fished it out of the canal behind the Hesketh last Sunday," she called back, deciding to miss that it was well past midnight with Damon after their candle shop Christmas party. "And we're waiting for the ice to melt." Claire let go of the fountain to shake back her sleeve where a watch would sit if she was more organised. "I'll be inside in a few hours?"

"Don't be ridiculous. Just get a move on and get in here. Anne's waiting to meet you, and she's rushed off her feet as it is." Janet backed into the conservatory, but her head poked out and she added, "And I hope you washed that trolley."

"I think you're right," Mark said as Janet rushed back into the house. "I think I know her already."

"Her bark is worse than her bite, I promise."

"We all have a teddy bear side, don't we?" Mark said, and she couldn't help but notice how closely he resembled a smiley, cuddly-looking bear. "And this part of the path isn't as bad as the part you slid down. Between the two of us, I think we can make it."

Following Mark's lead onto the ice, Claire copied his slow shuffles, barely lifting her feet. Mark was better equipped in walking boots. Her own trainers were smooth, perfect for dashing around the flat, iceless shop. Still, before long they were on the flat path at the side of the house, which someone had salted, thankfully.

Built of beige stone bricks, the two-centuries-old Starfall House stood alone at the bottom of Starfall Park. Both were named after the grand observatory on the hill, which always drew attention. If his accent hadn't given him away as not being from around these parts, the dazzled look in Mark's eyes as he gazed up to the observatory barely visible through the fog did.

"It's never open," Claire said, nodding at the giant 'FOR SALE' sign that jutted from the house as they reached the front. "Comes with the house, so if you want to buy it, you get it thrown in as a deal."

Mark gave a friendly smile, but the observatory had captured his interest. Leaving him standing outside the house, Claire pushed inside, glad to feel some warmth in the air. Looking around, she tugged off her gloves with her teeth, and the ends of her fingers prickled as the feeling rushed back into them.

Stalls dotted around the black and white tiled, richly decorated entrance hall sold everything from mulled wine to soap, wooden ornaments, and cards. Some were still in the middle of setting up, but most stallholders were lingering around, talking in groups. They were almost exclusively women and Claire's age or older. She smiled, glad she'd made it safely. She was excited for the day ahead.

Her mother stopped mopping at the base of the stairs and marched up to her.

"You don't have to thank me," Janet said, unravelling Claire's scarf from around her neck the moment she was close enough. "I paid the pitch fee already, so call it an early Christmas present. I got a decent discount, with Janet's Angels being hired to keep the place spic and span all weekend. This extravagant place has been a welcome treat compared to all the offices I clean during the week."

"I still don't understand how you got me a stall so easily. Did someone drop out?"

Janet shook her head, leaning in. "I was dumping my mop bucket outside at precisely the right time, or I might not have heard them talking about it."

"Heard who talking about what?"

"Anne and her assistant," Janet gestured over to the group of people crowded around one of the stalls, leaving

Claire no wiser to which, if any of them was Anne Evans, the elusive organiser of the craft fair. "The assistant was complaining to Anne that they hadn't filled all the stalls, but Anne was trying to tell her it didn't matter and that once word got around, they'd attract more stallholders. The assistant went off grumbling to herself."

"Her name is Kirsty," Mark said, appearing behind Claire; maybe she hadn't left him outside after all. "Kirsty Fisher. If you were to ask her, she planned this entire event down to the last detail, but given how distracted my mother has been lately, I don't know how much of her attention she's given to this fair. I trust she'll claim all the glory at the end of the day regardless."

"Distracted?" Janet said, her ears pricking up at the first hint of gossip. "Not important. What's important is that I got you into this craft fair, Claire. Did you *actually* apply?"

"Yes?" Claire couldn't help but laugh at the sudden accusation in her mother's voice. "As soon as I heard about it. My application was rejected almost immediately. I assumed all the stalls had been filled, but now that I'm looking around the room..." Of the ten or so in the entrance hall, at least three were empty. People weren't rushing in through the door despite precious set-up minutes ticking by. "Maybe there was an error with the system."

"All applications were checked by hand," Mark said. "I

helped, but I'm not sure I saw yours. Maybe there was an error? It is the first year, after all. My mother insists the whole thing will be a rip-roaring success, but I'll be happy if we get some people through the door on such a bitter day."

"You have to have more faith, Mark," a woman called, descending the staircase with a cardboard box hugged at her front. "You get your pessimism from your father."

Mark gave a smile as though he'd been caught out. "I'm sure the day will go swimmingly, Mother. I don't think you've met Claire. She's taking one of the empty stalls."

As Anne Evans passed them, the box she carried rattled in a way familiar to Claire. Anne placed the package on a half-finished stall of Christmas cards and knitted cup warmers and turned around with a tense smile. Chunky plastic jewellery clanged together at her wrists as her arms folded over her festive red poncho. As bright as her exterior was, the polite smile barely hid her open judgement. It was a look Claire knew all too well, thanks to her mother and the Women's Institute company she used to keep. The focus of Anne's squinting stare seemed to be the contents of the trolley Claire had risked her life to get delivered.

"Anne, this is my daughter, Claire, who I was telling you about," Janet said when Mark's attempt at an introduction didn't prompt anything. "Say 'hello', Claire."

"Hello, Claire," Claire said, holding out her hand. Anne's sour expression didn't move a muscle, and Claire continued, "Nice to meet you. I run the candle shop in the square. You might have seen it?"

Anne's hand and stare lingered like her son's, though Mark hadn't made Claire feel so scrutinised. "I've walked past it once or twice."

"Claire swears she applied for a stall and was rejected," Janet said in a speculative tone, as if Claire wasn't there. "Any chance she filled things in incorrectly?"

"Quite possibly," Anne said, turning her head as if distracted by something across the room. She waved to someone. "I'll have to check. There were quite a few applications to get through. Will you excuse me? My assistant seems to want me for something." Anne walked around the stall, bashing it with her hip. The wood gave a jolt and something within the box jangled. Unmistakably glass. "Claire, you can have Stall X."

Anne walked across the entrance with swift strides, giving the wet patch Janet had been mopping a wide berth. She joined a tall woman with a short fringe and a clipboard, and after talking amongst themselves for a moment, both glared in Claire's direction.

"I must apologise for my mother," Mark said, unzipping his coat to reveal a red and white knitted jumper, that matched the foiled labels of the candy cane candles in Claire's trolley. "She seems to have woken up on the wrong side of the bed. Happens a lot since Scott turned up on the scene." Mark glanced in the direction of the sweeping staircase in the centre of the entrance hall. "You should go and get set up. People will start arriving soon, hopefully."

"See you around?"

"Oh, I should think so," he said, flashing another apple-cheeked smile.

Mark let himself under a rope boundary tied across the bannisters, cutting off the staircase to the market. Claire wasn't sure where he was going or why he was headed upstairs, but she followed his journey to the landing.

"Quite a nice fella, don't you think?" Janet whispered in her ear. "Charming."

"I know *that* voice," Claire said. "Have you forgotten about Ryan? He's only been in Spain for two weeks. Do we need to get you into the doctors for a check-up?"

"I'm fit as a fiddle, dear." Janet swirled her mop around in the bucket and added, "And I was only saying. It's never a bad thing to have options."

Dumbfounded, Claire wondered what had happened to the woman who'd been beyond relieved to hear that Claire had entered her first adult relationship with her childhood friend, Ryan, in her mid-thirties.

Janet asked about a wedding every other week, so why the turnabout now? Her mother never said anything without intention, but before Claire could dig for deeper meaning, her father, Alan, walked in, his sunny smile the warmth to balance Janet's frosty edges.

"I heard there was a stall that needed an extra pair of hands," Alan said, hobbling inside with his cane, not that he was letting himself put as much pressure on it as he did in the house. "Where do you want me, little one?"

"Follow me," Claire said, pushing forward with the trolley as her mother swiped away the trails of gritty sludge following her. "X marks the spot."

Across the hall, Anne and the woman holding the clipboard – Kirsty Fisher, presumably – tracked her to the library. Given their lack of attempt to hide their obvious whispering, Claire was confident her application hadn't been lost, overlooked, or incorrectly filled in.

As much as she intended to make the most of the weekend ahead, Claire didn't feel all that welcome at Northash's first annual arts and crafts fair.

CHAPTER TWO

"*I*t sounds like things are busier here than there. Your candy cane candles are flying off the shelves." From the echo of Damon's voice, he'd stuck his head in the shop's back room, but she could hear the chatter of customers in the background. Claire wouldn't keep him long. "Lunchtime's coming up, so maybe you'll get a stampede?"

"Here's hoping." Claire peered around the column that blocked her view of the library. A few customers had filtered through, but nothing close to a stampede. "Not that it'll make any difference. You should see the stall she's given me. I'm crammed in a corner, hidden behind a column, and I'm the only person with an empty stall on either side. People keep walking on by. My dad's handing out samples to try and get people here. Turn left at Stall

R. If you reach J, you've gone too far. Return to Stall H and point to the clock. Take three paces west, and you might just notice Claire's Candles stuck in the back."

"Only a psycho would have alphabetical stalls and *not* have them in alphabetical order," he said. "I'm queasy just thinking about it."

"Yes, well, you might not be far off." Claire looked around the column. Her father was on the other side of the room, keeping three women entertained with some story he was telling them, a tray of samples held high. "Are you sure you don't know an Anne Evans? I thought she hated me when I first met her, but now, I'm certain. Whenever she comes into the room, I feel like I kicked her puppy or pushed her nan down the stairs."

"Just stare back at her."

"That's the thing, she's not staring. She's *blanking* me like I'm not here, and given where she's stuck me, I might as well not be." Claire exhaled. "I wish I knew what I'd done to her. Maybe she was a customer I upset?"

"Even if she was, we do a good job on that front. All our reviews say we're friendly and helpful." Damon sucked the air through his teeth, and a woman laughed jollily in the background, making Claire wish she was in her shop. "Maybe we worked with her at the candle factory up the hill? Quite a few Annes passed through during our years there."

Claire shook her head, adjusting one of her winter

forest candles atop a crate doubling as a display stand. "No. She's not from around here. She's posh. I'll let you get back to the shop. Someone's just walked in who might be able to tell me what's going on."

Claire hung up as Em Jones, the owner of Starfall House, crossed the library. Em immediately noticed Alan and made a beeline for him until she saw Claire. Her face lit up with surprise, and she headed straight for the column. Maybe Claire wasn't so invisible after all. Em's smile always lit up a room, her warm personality matching her bright clothes and many tattoos.

"I thought you couldn't get a stall?" Em gave Claire a comforting hug. "The smell of peppermint hits you right away. It's delicious. I don't doubt you'll sell out."

"Chance would be a fine thing," Claire said as Em pulled the lid from the candy cane candle. "Do you know much about the organiser, Anne? I feel like she's punishing me for something I don't know I've done."

"Anne Evans?" Em seemed surprised, though she didn't seem to disbelieve Claire. She placed the candle back carefully. "I'm somewhat good friends with Anne's friend, Carol. Carol Poole. She's in the drawing room selling her sculptures. She goes to many of the same yoga retreats I do, and when I told her about this house still being up for sale, she told me about Anne's situation. Anne recently came into a considerable amount of money and found herself between homes. She has been

17

looking for a large property like this one. I think they're from down near Oxford or that way about."

"You've sold the house? That's great news!" Claire said. Em was the most unlikely homeowner, more suited to her simple, frugal life living on a canal narrowboat.

"Not quite yet, but I think I might be able to unburden myself of this place soon. Anne seems eager." Em looked around as though she could still feel lingering ghosts from the events that led to her inheriting the house from her grandmother, Opal. Claire certainly could. "Anne asked if she could rent rooms here to test drive the place, and I can't say I blame her. A house like this is a big commitment. I expected her to come alone, but she brought a whole group with her, which I didn't mind. The rent money is helping with the mounting overheads, which your estate agent friend, Sally, has been wonderful in helping to manage. Anne's been dealing with Sally mostly, but I pop by now and then. She's always been pleasant enough. What has she done to make you think she's punishing you?"

"Call it a feeling," Claire said, sighing. "I just can't help but feel this is personal."

"You might be right," the woman at the clothes stall one empty table over said, leaning in. Bianca, according to her 'Bianca's Boutique' banner. "I couldn't help but overhear. I've known Anne for years, and that sounds like exactly something she'd do. She'd cut off her nose to spite her face. Not that it's any of my business."

Bianca, a woman in her forties with sleek, ice-blonde hair, retreated into her stall filled with bags, shoes, and jewellery. She'd seemed deep in thought since Claire had set up near her, not noticing – or ignoring – Claire's attempts to catch her eye to introduce herself.

"These lovely ladies would like to purchase some candles," Alan said brightly, bringing over two women already carrying bags from other stalls. "Black cherry for Sherry and winter pine for Caroline."

"I'll leave them in your capable hands, Dad," Claire said, plucking a candy cane candle from the table. "I need to go and speak to Anne about something."

"Are you sure that's wise, dear?" Alan asked, maintaining his broad smile as the women busied themselves plucking out full-sized candles to sample. "Perhaps wait until after lunch?"

"We're all adults. I won't be long."

Claire had never been one for confrontation, but she'd also never been one for childish games. Like she'd told her father, they were all adults. Anne had at least thirty years on her, but given where they both were, Claire already knew they had one thing in common. They shared a love of crafting.

She walked through the archway to the entrance hall, where most customers congregated. Many were in front of the stall Claire assumed belonged to Anne. She couldn't see the woman but could hear her, thanks to her chunky jewellery. Claire hung back and decided to wait for the throng to clear.

"Can I help you?"

Kirsty, the assistant with the short fringe and clipboard, approached Claire. Their haircuts weren't dissimilar, cut blunt and neat just above their shoulders. Still, Kirsty's fringe was a good two inches shorter than Claire's. It resembled the fringe Claire's mother would sometimes cut with kitchen scissors and a promise she'd 'grow into it.' What Kirsty didn't have in hair inches, she made up for in height. It didn't take much for Claire to feel short, but she rarely had to crane her neck so high for another woman.

"I was just wanting to talk to Anne."

"Is it about your stall?" Kirsty's smile was plastered on, her eyes blank, as though she'd already anticipated and troubleshot Claire's question. "She's rather busy right now, but I'd be happy to talk to you about any issues you have."

Claire tiptoed, catching the top of Anne's head.

"Why was my application for a stall rejected?"

"I'm sorry, I'm not at liberty to discuss that."

Claire arched a brow at the woman, wondering if her seriousness *was* serious, but her expression didn't falter. Knowing the assistant would do nothing but stonewall, Claire conceded. She wandered to the less busy stall next to Anne's selling sweet, scented bath bombs and spiced soaps, all in Christmas shapes. Claire picked up a bar of cinnamon-infused soap in the form of a snowman, her eyes firmly on Anne, whose customers were keeping her busy. She seemed to have the prime spot by the door to catch people coming and going.

Claire wanted to get to the bottom of things for the sake of peace, not war. Clutching her candle, Claire slipped between the stalls and joined Anne behind hers. Anne glared at her, and Claire noticed how, like Mark's, her eyes were a sparkling blue. She hadn't noticed the colour during their first meeting, but then, she hadn't seen the red rings – as though she'd recently been crying – around her eyes, either.

"What are you doing here?" Anne asked, not stopping counting out change from a metal cash box. "Get back to your own stall. I'm busy. *Kirsty?*"

"I've brought you one of my candles in hopes of…"

Claire looked down at Anne's stall and realised why the clattering box Anne had carried downstairs sounded so familiar. She heard the same sound several times a day as she ferried candles from the storeroom to the shop front. Half of Anne's stall was still taken up by the Christmas cards and knitted mug warmers, but the other half was filled with candles.

"You're selling candles too," Claire said, the words slipping out. "You didn't want the competition."

Claire had spoken quietly and was sure the customers were too busy in their consumer bubbles to hear. But from the abrupt temper in Anne's red-ringed eyes, Claire knew she'd said the quiet part out loud.

"*Excuse* me?" Anne said, twice as loud as Claire, quietening some of the buzz. "Are you saying I don't think my candles are good enough to sell?"

Claire narrowed her eyes at the woman. Anne's angry glare was so tight she looked like she'd pop a blood vessel any moment. Surely Claire's comment hadn't caused such a reaction? Not on its own.

"That's not what I said." Claire maintained her calm, knowing her intentions. She held out the candle. "It seems we have a passion in common. I'm sure there'll be enough customers to go around, though, if I'd be able to move stalls—"

"So, now you're accusing me of *sabotaging* you?"

"I wasn't. But now that you've said it, I have to wonder," she said, to which some people gasped. Claire looked around, and from the glares, they were on Anne's side. "This is silly. I came over here to give you a candle and figure out if we had some common ground, and—"

Fingers closed tightly around Claire's shoulder. She spun around instinctively, batting away the hand that belonged to Kirsty. Claire's hip bumped the stall, jolting it forward. It was a gentle tap, but the candles lurched. A woman at the front of the stall stumbled back, and another nudged her right back into the table. The candles jumped, and this time, so did the tabletop. The jars crashed down to the black and white tiles in a cascade that nobody could stop. After the last candle smashed, silence fell on Starfall House.

"*You!*" Anne growled at Claire. "You came here to accuse *me* of sabotage, yet that's exactly what you have done. You've destroyed my stall!"

"I barely bumped it," Claire said, hearing the defence in her voice as she searched the crowd for someone to back her up. The woman whose lurch had sent it tumbling had gone. "It's not fair to—"

"*Fair?*" Anne cried. "I want you out of here, now. Look at what you've done!"

"Steady on, Mother," Mark's voice came from somewhere in the crowd. "I'm sure it was just an accident."

"Months of work," Anne said, staring blankly at her destroyed stall. She exhaled, letting the tension vanish from her shoulders. "I'm going up to my room. Kirsty, will you see to it that this is cleaned up?"

"Of course, Anne."

Head down, Anne left the scene of the shove and took the stairs with heavy steps. It was like no one dared speak until she was behind her bedroom door, but the second she disappeared, the whispering spread, and all eyes turned to Claire.

"I don't think you should be here when Anne gets back," Kirsty said when she returned with a brush and shovel. "You've done enough damage."

"Now, just wait a minute!" Janet barged through the crowd and planted herself by Claire's side. "I won't have you accusing my daughter of something like that. From where I was standing, Anne was the one ranting and raving."

But Claire knew it didn't matter how she'd acted. Anne had spoken the loudest, spinning a narrative that had stuck with the people closest, judging by their stony stares. She'd doubted her decision to rush to the fair before the disaster at Anne's table, but now Claire wanted nothing more than to be back in the safe bubble of her shop, with Damon, having her first coffee all over again, accompanied by cheesy Christmas music on the radio.

"Thanks for getting me through the door," Claire said to her mother as Kirsty swept around her. "I'd say I've outstayed my welcome, but I don't think I ever had one."

Kirsty was doing her best impression of someone pretending she couldn't hear Claire, despite being so close. She shimmied the table legs from under the mess of wood and glass and leaned them against the wall.

"The screws?" Claire asked Kirsty directly.

"I'm sorry?"

"For the table legs." Claire tapped a finger on the leg of the table selling the soap and bath bombs. "Where are the screws that should have kept this all together?"

"Oh." Kirsty flicked a few large pieces of glass around in the mountain she'd pushed into the shovel. "They're probably amongst all this. Really, I don't think it's a good idea for you to be here when Anne returns. She's already having a tough enough day."

"Yes, I got that feeling," Claire said, staring at the empty holes drilled into the wood. "Do keep an eye out for those screws. If you don't find them, Anne might not have been too far off about being sabotaged – though it certainly wasn't me."

CHAPTER THREE

he whispering and stares followed Claire back to the shop. She'd hoped the craft fair would increase footfall, and it had. What small business owner wouldn't love a full shop? Yet she'd have happily locked the doors and hid in her flat until the fair was over. She might even have done so if not for Damon pulling her through the day. One of the many benefits of having one of her closest friends working alongside her.

"Cheer up, mate," Damon said to her later that night in their usual corner of The Hesketh Arms. They were the furthest from the crackling fire and the Christmas tree where people tended to congregate. It was always busy around Christmas, and as usual, the place had been smothered in decorations. "It's not like you to push food around on your plate. You love The Hesketh's Christmas dinner. We have about ten a year. It's genius to serve it all of December." Damon crammed a fork stacked with turkey, sprouts, and cranberry sauce into his mouth. "You can't let one woman ruin your entire day. People aren't staring at you."

"I never said they were."

"You keep glancing over your shoulder. You've been jumping at the shadows all day."

Claire did it again, scanning the bar while Wham! sang about 'Last Christmas'. The craft fair had ended for the day around the time they'd shut up the shop. They'd seen the sea of women flowing from the park down into the village, splitting off between The Park Inn and The Hesketh with their paper bags. Most of the tables had those bags on them, and eyes from all those tables glanced at Claire as she scanned the room.

"It *feels* like they are," she said, stabbing a sprout. "You know what it's like 'round here. Whoever screams loudest gets the last word."

"Only to idiots," he said. "*You* know the truth. You might have knocked the table, but you didn't take the screws out. Forget what everyone else thinks."

"I'm not just thinking about me. I'm thinking about the shop too," she said, looking in its direction, though it was hidden behind a wall flashing with a curtain of twinkling lights. "We've only just got over our autumn slump, and now there are only two weeks to go until the big day. If this sticks, it will be the bone in the turkey sandwich to ruin our Christmas sales."

"The shop is doing fine," Damon said reassuringly. "I'm on top of the numbers. Online sales from our new site are trickling in, and we had a full shop today."

"Didn't feel like we sold much."

"We did just fine." He offered her a tight smile. "Besides, you should be the one supporting me tonight. So, you were publicly humiliated at the craft fair. Big whoop." He winked, and they both laughed. "I'm the one meeting Sally's mum tonight. Sally seems terrified, which is making me terrified. Is she awful?"

"No?" Claire answered, hearing the uncertainty. "Eileen is just … direct. Let's just say she never tried to hide that she thought I was less than smart compared to Sally. It's always with a smile, though. Can't tell if that's better or worse."

"Definitely worse." It was Damon's turn to push his food around his plate. "This is what I get for waiting until this age for my first serious relationship. I've never met anyone's parents before. It's a big step. I won't lie … I'm bricking it. What if she hates me?"

"She probably will," Claire said, offering him a supportive smile, "but don't take it personally. I think she hates everyone. Sally will be there. After tonight, it's just Christmas and birthdays. That's how I think about my Grandma Moreen."

"Is Mean Moreen invited for Christmas after what happened?"

Claire glanced to the spot in the pub where Janet and her mother, Moreen, had confronted each other after years of built-up tension, primarily harboured by Janet. Mean Moreen, whose biting tongue and cold presence had earned her the fitting name, hadn't been heard from since, and Janet had been all the lighter for it.

"My mum hasn't brought her up," Claire said. "I'll have to ask. And just for the record, I still don't think it's fair. Either Anne didn't set her table up correctly, or somebody took the screws out. Anne shouldn't get to—"

"Please, Claire," Damon interrupted with a dead-eyed stare. Fair enough, she thought. He'd been the one having to listen to her all day. "You can't prove it either way. It'll only eat you up. When's Ryan home?"

Claire was glad of the distraction. For the first time all day, she took a relaxing breath that had some effect. "His flight gets into Manchester tonight."

Damon sipped his pint, and Claire did the same. "Has he found her?"

The Hesketh homebrew jammed in Claire's throat, knowing who he was referring to. She wondered if he was sparing her having to hear the name of her boyfriend's estranged wife.

"Maya?" Claire confirmed anyway. Damon nodded. "When he calls, I can tell it's the last thing he wants to talk about, so I just leave it be. He went out there to find her and get the divorce wheels rolling, and I've taken a step back to give him the space to do that. It's hardly the norm, is it?"

"And yet we find ourselves in a similar situation after being similarly single as long as we were. My mum kept telling me, 'You just wait until you get to your thirties and forties when all the divorces start happening. That's when you'll finally get a girlfriend', and for once, she might have been right. Since Sally and Paul reached their divorce settlement, she's been like a new woman. That was, until Eileen's insistence that she meet 'the new one.' Her words." He ate the final piece of turkey and pushed his plate away. "Still, after tonight, I'll know if I'm going to survive meeting my future mother-in-law, and you're going to know the score with Ryan and Maya. Plenty to keep our minds occupied, wouldn't you say?"

Claire got the subtle 'don't think about Anne' hint. Homebrew still in hand, she took another sip as the excitement of seeing Ryan bubbled up inside her. When Claire had waved Ryan and the kids off at the airport two weeks ago, he'd been hopeful that he'd return with a resolution to the whereabouts of his estranged wife. He hadn't promised he'd be able to track her down, but she'd seen the fire in his eyes. She'd heard that fire fizzle out in his voice during their phone calls over the past two weeks.

"Wish me luck." Damon finished his pint and grabbed his coat. "And remember that people have short memories around here. Today's gossip is tomorrow's 'what happened again?'"

Claire rose to leave with him, not wanting to stick around with the target Anne had painted on her back. She bumped the table with her thighs, clattering the cutlery. Claire knew she didn't imagine the subtle pause in the conversations around her. A glance over her shoulder confirmed the same whispering she'd seen from Anne and Kirsty.

It hadn't hurt much then. Maybe because she'd thought she could sort things out. Now, it stung. They loved making crafts or buying them, which was where most crafters started. It's where Claire began. She'd been looking forward to some shopping at the fair, not having been to one since she'd opened her own shop. They were supposed to be her people, but she felt they were impatiently waiting for the 'woman flips table' act at the circus.

"Ah, Claire, there you are!" The chill-bitten cheeks of Eugene beamed out at her on her way to the door. "I've just been to your shop. Love the new window display. You've really captured the season. I was wondering if I could have a word?"

Once again, Claire felt a hush fall around her. How much were their ears straining? Eugene must have noticed it too. He held open the door for her, and they shut themselves in the vestibule.

"Now, I know this isn't true, so I wanted you to hear this from a friend if you haven't already," Eugene said, his usually booming voice taking on a surprising softness. "I was helping Marley in the café today, and I overheard *several* people accusing the candles in your shop of being ... factory bought."

The words hit Claire with the intended drama. A slap across the face, a kick in the gut, and – after years working in a candle factory – one of the worst things she could hear.

Eugene rested a supportive hand on her shoulder when her response didn't come. "I, of course, set each and every one of them straight. I've seen you making them in the back of your shop with my own two eyes. Being a former politician, I know what it's like to be the subject of a smear campaign. I wanted to arm you with this information, though I'm afraid I don't know the source."

"I think I do," Claire said, reaching for the door. "Thank you so much, Eugene. I appreciate you bringing this to me. Your next candle is on me."

"Then I shall see you bright and early tomorrow, and don't let the buggers get you down."

Leaving Eugene in the pub, Claire walked out into the night. The cold air was refreshing after the stuffy atmosphere in the pub. Hands in her pockets, she passed the clock tower, and her shop came into view. Its frosty, brilliant-white and fire-engine-red window display, created using layers of translucent plastic, carefully placed lighting, and fake snow, was a bright spark pop in the otherwise traditional window displays of her fellow shopkeepers. The chippy had trimmed the window in tinsel, and the greengrocers had thrown a little spray-on snow in the corners of the windows. The post office and butcher on either corner hadn't bothered with anything.

A window display was only half the story when it came to getting people through the door. If it caught the eyes of the right people, an online post could send a short burst of customers flooding through the door. With an active smear campaign, it would take having Father Christmas himself sitting in the window for the rumours from Starfall House not to matter. Wholly undeserved, at that.

Claire looked up to the window of her flat's living room, where one of her cats, Domino, was staring out, following something with her eyes. A fly, no doubt. They could wait another fifteen minutes for their dinner.

How did Damon expect her not to think about Anne?

Anne Evans couldn't get away with lying about her, regardless of if she was having a bad day. The more Claire thought about Anne's blue eyes with their red rings, the more she'd been convinced Anne had spent considerable time between their two meetings crying.

She'd have noticed if her eyes had been that raw when they'd met. It wasn't fair that Anne was taking it out whatever had happened on Claire and her business.

She had to set the record straight, and there was only one way to do it – by going to the source.

———

As cold as it was in the park, Claire found herself lingering outside the front doors of Starfall House longer than she'd intended to. With the right company, the moon above the fog might have been romantic, but alone, it was unsettling.

Through the mist on the hill, she noticed the lights were on in the observatory. A rare occurrence – and they hadn't been on when she'd entered the park.

Staring up at the large window above the front door, Claire could almost see Opal Jones. Frail fingers curled over the arms of a wheelchair, pale eyes only able to see the light and shade, thin white hair wispy against the sun. As weak as Opal had looked, she'd been clued into her loyal housekeeper's plan to kill her for the inheritance. Opal's final trick had been to leave the house to her estranged granddaughter, Em – the last person who wanted it.

A camera flashed, and Claire's eyes re-adjusted. Mark was looking down at her from the darkness caused by the heavy curtains. He held up a hand, his other holding his camera. She returned the wave, though she couldn't ignore how unsettled she felt. How long had he been standing there?

Claire pushed into the house after finding the front door unlocked. She expected to be met by Mark, but silence greeted her. There wasn't a single light on in the place. Without the stallholders, the tables, all laid out in the dark with their lovingly crafted items, looked abandoned. The table had been replaced at Anne's stall and was fully stocked and ready for the following day. Given how busy the market was reported to have been by late afternoon, the mishap with the table hadn't come close to wiping out Anne's inventory. Her histrionics had suggested otherwise.

"Hello?" Claire called out, turning into the library. "Anyone here?"

Her voice echoed back to her. She squinted into the dark. Stall X had vanished from behind the column. Maybe they'd taken it for Anne's replacement, or perhaps she couldn't bear looking at it. Seemed ridiculous, but most of Anne's actions – or, rather, overreactions – had been so far.

Claire doubled back to the entrance hall and spotted something that made her crouch. It was one of her candles. The label was face down against the black tile, but from the white wax and the sweet peppermint scent alone, she knew it was her new candy cane creation. She reached out, but her hand stopped before it touched the glass. The edges of the tile bled out into the surrounding white tiles, disturbing the chequered formation.

Claire heard her father's voice in her head. Not the kindly man with the cane who'd used his gift of the gab to sell more candles than Claire during her short hours at the fair. It was the firm and sure voice of the retired detective inspector that came out when a certain level of seriousness was needed.

Don't touch a thing, Claire, the voice ordered.

Claire tugged her hand back and went for the phone in her pocket, just as the grand chandelier above her sparked to life, illuminating what she'd hoped she wouldn't find. The candle was lying in smeared blood. A shrill scream dragged her up to her feet.

Kirsty stood in the doorway to the kitchen in a thick, padded coat. She was half-bent and screaming, her eyes flicking from Claire to the source of what had disturbed her.

Anne lay at the foot of the staircase, her blue eyes colder than ever. Kirsty's arm reached up, pointing at Claire as her screams brought people out of the rooms on the landing above.

Claire's stomach sank.

How am I going to explain this one?

"Explain this to me again," DI Ramsbottom said, pausing his pacing of the kitchen to peek through the door to the entrance hall. The place was swarming with officials. "And please, try to speak as slowly as possible this time."

"I came back from a walk around the park to clear my head," Kirsty said in a small voice, sitting across from Claire at the kitchen table. Mark was also in the room, though he hadn't said much; his stunned expression spoke clearly enough. "I walked into the entrance hall, turned on the light, and the first thing I saw was *that* woman," – she paused to point at Claire again – "putting the candle she killed Anne with on the ground."

"That's not quite how things happened," Claire offered, sipping the tea Ramsbottom had thrust upon her. By the taste of it, he'd dumped in half a cup of sugar. Maybe it would help with the shake in her hands. "I wasn't putting the jar down. I didn't even touch it. Well, not at that moment, at least."

"She keeps changing her story," Kirsty said, flapping her finger at Claire. "One minute she says she didn't touch it, and now she might have touched it. Which is it?"

"Give it a rest, Kirsty." Mark kicked away from the wall and took the last remaining chair at the table. "Of course, there's a chance Claire touched the candle at some point. She made it. We all saw her holding one of them when that table fell over. Put your brain to good use and think about what you're saying."

Hearing herself defended felt like a gulp of fresh air through the hand of perception gripped around Claire's throat.

"Claire?" Ramsbottom scratched his stiff, shiny hair with the end of his pen. "Care to shed some light on the situation?"

"At the pub, I heard that someone was spreading rumours about my candles," Claire said, struggling to find her voice. "I came here to try and put things to bed with Anne. She's been painting me as something I'm not. I was trying to find a bridge where I could meet her halfway."

"You knocked down her table," Kirsty said, stamping the wagging finger down on the table top. "Everyone saw you."

"Did you find those screws?"

"No," Kirsty said triumphantly. "Funny that you knew they were missing. You must have been the one to take them out."

"I knew because the table fell down like it was being held together by the sheer power of hope," Claire said, raising her voice to match Kirsty's. "I arrived after everyone else. If I had taken the screws, somebody would have seen me. It was the busiest place in the market."

"Smell her breath." Kirsty's finger stretched out again

in pointed accusation. "She's been drinking. I bet she doesn't know what she did or didn't do."

"I had half a pint with my dinner at the pub," Claire said, unable not to laugh. "What are you? My mother? Like I said, I came straight here from the pub. Anne was already dead when I arrived."

"Why were you creeping around in the dark then?" Kirsty's hand slammed down on the table. "Answer that."

"How would I know where the light switches are? I recognised my candle on the ground and was about to pull out my phone flash when you walked in and turned on the lights. I saw Anne at the *same* time you did."

"You have an answer for everything," Kirsty said dismissively. "I know what I saw."

"Perhaps she has an answer for everything because it's the truth," Mark offered, spreading his hands wide. "I don't for one second believe Claire removed the screws from my mother's table, and I also know she arrived here tonight only a minute before you screamed the house down. Hardly time enough for an altercation followed by a murder."

Mark's logic was sound and seemed to bring a little calm to the edge in the room. Claire was glad he was there to balance out Kirsty, but she understood Kirsty's emotional outburst. She'd just found her boss dead. Mark had been one of the first Kirsty's wails had summoned, and he'd been as cool as a cucumber, barely showing any emotion since first seeing his mother's dead body at the foot of the stairs.

"Mark took a picture of me," Claire thought aloud. "Evidence of the time I arrived."

"I'll need a copy of that," Ramsbottom said.

Mark nodded, bowing his head a little. He cleared his throat, his cheeks reddening. Claire wondered if he'd meant to take the picture with the flash off. The door to the conservatory opened, and a gust of icy wind came in.

A short woman in tight running clothes, with the slight frame of a child and the lined skin of someone past retirement, entered the kitchen, pulling down a hood. She had short grey hair, swept over a little like the golden mop on Ramsbottom's head. If Kirsty was one of the tallest women Claire had met, the newcomer had to be one of the shortest, and Claire came from a long line of short Harris women on Granny Greta's side. The woman looked around the room, her brows arching as she picked up on the mood.

"What's happened?"

"Something awful," Kirsty said. "You might want to sit down, Carol."

Carol Poole, Anne's friend and the sculptor Em had told her about. Carol shrugged off her coat to reveal veiny, muscly arms with little body fat. She looked like someone Claire expected to find hanging around a yoga retreat. Carol took a seat, and Claire rose from hers simultaneously. She wasn't sure she had the energy for more high emotion, especially with someone in the room determined to undermine her every word.

"We can finish this interview at the police station, Detective Inspector," Claire said, holding open the door to the conservatory. "As a person of interest, I'm happy to comply with your investigation and tell you the truth somewhere else."

"Right you are," he said, hurrying to the door with a snap of his heels. "You know, you might be the first person who's asked to be brought in. Not guilty, are you, Claire?"

Claire sighed, unsure if he was expecting her to answer. She had never anticipated being the subject of conspiracies in her own village, but in half a day, she'd gone from being accused of sabotaging a table, defrauding her customers by buying her candles from a factory, and now, worst of all, murder.

All three snowballs had landed exactly where they'd meant to. If someone was trying to frame her, they were doing a great job so far.

CHAPTER FOUR

*C*laire blinked along with the lights changing colour on the other side of the frosted window of the interview room. Blue. Green. Red. Yellow. In one of the houses near the cottage police station, someone was blasting Mariah Carey's Christmas album. The record was on its third spin – Claire's only way of measuring the passing time. Confession forced by Christmas music torture. She wondered if it was part of the station's interrogation tactics.

As mad it was driving her, Claire couldn't confess to something she hadn't done. Lights aside, her mind hadn't wandered away from what had happened at Starfall for a second. The candle in the blood next to the body at the bottom of the stairs.

Anne hadn't been pushed or fallen.

She'd been lying too neatly, arms by her sides, eyes pointing up to stare into the great beyond. From what Claire had seen, she'd had a wound at the back of her head, but there hadn't been much blood. Like Mariah, Claire didn't want much for Christmas either.

Just a redo of the day.

"Sorry to keep you waiting, Claire," Detective Inspector Harry Ramsbottom bustled into the room, a steaming cup in each hand, a folder crammed under his arm. "The damn printer was playing up, but when aren't they?" He plopped the plastic cup in front of her. "Hot chocolate from the vending machine. We've been meaning to get the heating fixed, but ... budget."

Ramsbottom dropped into the chair across from her as Claire peered into the lumpy, grey surface of the supposed hot chocolate with the consistency of tap water. She tugged her hands from her pockets and curled her fingers around the cup as Ramsbottom dug through the file, already knowing it would taste of nothing. Since entering the station, her gut instinct continued to talk in her father's voice.

Watch your words, Claire.

As eager as she was to know what was going on, she waited for Ramsbottom to make the first move.

"This is you arriving at the manor at 6:46 pm this evening," Ramsbottom said, laying out a black and white photograph. "The tech team are checking the validity of the time stamps as we speak. Quite artistic."

Artistic was one word for it. Claire's head poked up at the bottom of the picture, stretched out from the messed-up perspective. With the flash bouncing off the window, Claire glowed silver like a spectre, as though the image had been captured through Opal Jones's eyes. The subject of the image, however, wasn't Claire at all. Centred in the middle, beyond the bandstand and scattered trees, the lens had focused on the observatory, lit up. Claire felt a little settled. Maybe Mark hadn't been at the window taking secretive pictures of her.

"So," Ramsbottom said, looping his fingers, "we know when you arrived, and we logged Kirsty's frantic call at 6:48 pm three minutes later, which corroborates the story of Anne's son." He consulted his notes. "Mark Wood. Thirty-eight. He pointed out there wasn't much time for an altercation unless you walked in and hit her over the head without pausing."

"Do you really think I'm capable of that?" Claire took a sip. She'd been right. It was a cup of boiling hot nothing. "You've known me since I was a kid."

"Since your mother was pregnant with you," he said, gulping down half the hot chocolate in one squeeze of the plastic cup. Brown drops landed on his white shirt, adding to what looked like a ketchup stain. "Kirsty seems quite sure of what she saw, but I know things aren't always as they seem, which is why you're not under arrest. But I need your help understanding why your name is so connected to Anne Evans. I heard people talking about what happened at the craft fair. Is it true you flipped over her table and Kirsty had to restrain you?"

"It's a wild exaggeration of what happened, and I wouldn't be surprised if Anne was the one egging it on after I left." Claire took a calming breath; she almost wished she'd gone to the café for her lunch instead of the chippy and heard the wild stories about her. "I applied for the fair but didn't get in. I assumed they were full and didn't think much of it. But they weren't full, and my mum managed to get me a table. I could feel Anne didn't want me there from the moment we met. I thought perhaps we'd met before, but it wasn't me. It was my candles."

"And this is what the table-flipping was about?"

"Table *nudging*," Claire corrected. "The table didn't have any screws in it. Maybe it was an oversight or they thought they could get away with not needing them, but the tables around had screws. Someone took them out. I don't think I was the only person on Anne's naughty list today. The way she exploded at me, it felt like she was channelling her rage. It only made me think I was right about her dislike of me boiling down to the simple fact that we were both selling candles."

"Hardly worth killing over."

"Because I didn't kill her," Claire said, clenching her jaw to suppress the urge to reach across the table and shake some sense into the DI. "It sounds silly because it is silly. I went to her stall with a peace offering. I saw her candles and spoke before thinking, but nobody heard me. It wasn't a scene until she made it one. I might be the public face of Anne's enemies, but I promise you, Detective, I didn't kill her."

"There *were* quite a few people at the scene this evening," Ramsbottom said, consulting his notes. "I spoke to Mark, and Kirsty."

"There's also Anne's friend, Carol Poole," Claire remembered aloud. "She was the short lady who came in before we left. And Mark said there was a man called Scott."

"Ah, Scott Harper." Ramsbottom flicked back a page. "Anne's boyfriend. Perhaps they can paint a better picture of Anne. I'll have to ask them all to stick around. They're a bit posh for these parts, don't you think?"

Ramsbottom's voice suddenly took on a lighter tone, and Claire relaxed a little in the stiff plastic seat.

"Em, the homeowner, mentioned Anne renting a room and bringing some people with her," Claire offered. "Her son, her boyfriend, her assistant, that's a better place to start than with—"

A sharp, short knock at the door cut Claire off.

Another suited station member leaned into the room, handing a sheet of white paper to Ramsbottom. He took in the contents before letting out a sigh.

"You're free to go, Claire," Ramsbottom said, finally smiling, and she realised she hadn't been the only one holding tension in her chair. "Time of death is estimated to be between 5 pm and 5:30 pm."

"Which puts me in the shop."

"And we've already confirmed your alibi with your employee, Damon Gilbert." Ramsbottom consulted the pad again, scribbling an addition. "Your father's out-front waiting for you. He's been here all night."

Skidding her chair against the tiles, Claire looked at the Christmas lights one last time. Mariah had finally stopped. She left the interview room and walked down the bright corridor to the front of the station, where her father greeted her with a hug. Over his shoulder, the clock amongst the many posters brandishing slogans about knife crime and encouraging people to spy on their neighbours ticked past ten.

"I hope they treated you properly," Alan said to the room, standing tall as he looked around the station to awkward smiles and evasive eyes. She scanned for his cane, but it wasn't there. "C'mon, little one. Let's get you home. You've been here long enough."

THESE DAYS, 'HOME' TO CLAIRE MEANT THE FLAT ABOVE her shop, but after discovering that her dad had used his emergency key to feed the cats, Claire was happy when he drove her to the cul-de-sac she'd grown up in.

The warmth of her parents' hallway hugged her through the layers she'd left on throughout her stay at the station. She could smell her toffee apple candle burning somewhere, which had ended up being autumn's biggest seller after a slow start. So much so that she'd entirely sold out of her first two batches, and with a new 'cinnamon apple cider' label, it had snuck its way into her Christmas range. They'd have sold themselves with a good spot at a *fair* craft fair.

Before the disappointment over how the day had gone could take over, Ryan appeared in the kitchen at the end of the hall. A shaky smile pulled deep dimples into his cheeks. Usually pale, they'd taken on the golden hue they'd had when he'd first returned to Northash, as had his sandy red hair.

Abandoning unravelling her scarf, Claire met him in a hug halfway down the hallway. His hand cupped the back of her head as her face rested on his firm chest, and the two weeks that had felt like two months melted away. For that moment in Ryan's arms, everything was fine again.

"Claire?" her mother's voice broke through the peace, appearing from the sitting room, followed by Granny

Greta. "Oh, you're back. We've heard terrible things. What happened?"

"There's time for that, Janet," Greta said, shuffling Janet down the hall into the kitchen, patting Claire's cheek as she passed. "Let's give them some space."

Claire followed Ryan into the sitting room, where it seemed Janet and Greta had been indulging in a spot of Alan's whisky. She hoped they hadn't been worrying too much. Even at her light-blinking lowest, she'd known the police couldn't charge her with anything. She had the truth and an iron-clad alibi on her side. Sitting in the middle of the sofa, she told all of this to Ryan.

Ryan looked as tired as she felt, reminding her of the feeling of loss that had been shrinking since seeing his face in the hallway. She tossed back the quarter an inch of whisky in the nearest glass, resting on a coaster atop a women's magazine that promised to shave 'fifteen years off with fifteen minutes for fifteen days!'

"I'm sure it'll sort itself out," Claire said in a reassuring voice her own ears didn't believe. "I'm sorry this is what you've had to come home to. I thought I'd be coming to meet you at the airport. Funny how things turn out."

"I had texts from your mother crashing my phone from the second I turned it back on going through passport control," he said, clenching her hands in his. "We went to the station. Your mum and Greta were there too. We waited, but the kids were tired from travelling, so I took them home. Em's watching them." He glanced at the clock on the mantlepiece. "I really missed you, Claire."

Claire gripped his hands and moved in closer. The hint of apology in his voice made her uneasy. With the whisky sitting funnily in her stomach, she wondered how best to point out the elephant in the room.

"So," she started, "did you find her?"

Claire knew she sounded like Damon asking the same question earlier. So much for Damon's promise that it would be the only thing to focus on all night. She hoped his meeting with Eileen fared better.

"I didn't find Maya," Ryan said, bowing his head. "I thought I got close a couple of times, but every cousin, aunt, or friend pointed us in a different direction. I spent two weeks on a wild-goose-chase tour of my in-laws, but none of them could give me concrete information. It was good for the kids to see their family again, but … I can't help but feel like they were all covering for Maya. They know where she is, but they're protecting her." Ryan stood up suddenly and walked over to the window. Pulling back the curtains, he said, "I'm sorry, Claire. I thought I'd be coming home with a resolution. I wanted to knock this on the head so we could move forward."

Claire joined him at the window and rested her head on his arm. "You don't owe me an apology. You didn't know where she was before you left either, and I was fine with how we were."

"Yeah, me too." His arm slipped around her shoulder. "Going back to all those places again, remembering how things were…" Ryan's voice trailed off. He rarely talked about the time he was away living in Spain. "I'll admit, I'd rather swap the weather, but it feels good to be home. I don't know how I spent so long away." He pulled away from Claire and turned to the clock. "I need to get home to the kids. Em's already been with them for hours. Can we walk down together?"

"I think I'll stay here for a while," she said, returning for another hug. "See you tomorrow?"

"Lunch at mine?"

"It's a date." They shared a kiss. "You can tell me all about what happened in Spain, and hopefully by then the police will have arrested whoever killed Anne."

Alone in the sitting room, Claire tugged the curtain and looked off to the hill at Starfall Park. She wouldn't have been able to make out the park, a dark spot in the surrounding house and streetlights, but the observatory was still lighting up the night. The lit-up observatory had seemed odd then. Now, it was just another of the strange things to have happened in a day she'd happily reset.

"I've been patient, Claire," her mother called from the kitchen. "Time to talk."

AND TALK CLAIRE DID. WITH HER FATHER IN THE computer room in the house's box bedroom, Claire talked her mother and granny through the day. DI Ramsbottom's interrogation felt like a light-hearted snowball fight compared to her mother's pelted questions.

"And you definitely didn't snap?" Janet asked, firmly. "She *did* humiliate you in front of everyone."

"She *tried* to," Claire corrected. "Personally, I thought she humiliated herself more than me. I should have kept my mouth shut and stayed in my corner."

"When has a Harris woman ever done that?" Greta shot her a wink. "Give the woman some air, Janet. You know Claire didn't kill her. You'd believe the gossip over your own daughter?"

"Of course not, Greta." Janet pursed her lips. "But seemingly ordinary people can do terrible things, as we as a family know all too well."

Claire winced, knowing her mother was referring to Uncle Pat. Greta finished her whisky, and Claire wondered if that was to occupy her mouth from saying what she felt. It wasn't like they hadn't faced what Uncle Pat had done. Having a murderer behind bars in the family was a pill that wouldn't ever be entirely swallowed. Still, Claire questioned her mother's timing of the bomb.

"I'm sorry, love," Janet said in a quieter voice. "It's

been a stressful day for all of us. I know you've told us the truth. Let's hope they put this to bed before it sticks."

"And stick it will," Greta said, unscrewing the bottle's cap. "The things I've been hearing today … my voice is hoarse from defending you, Claire. They've created a complete fiction."

"Based on a dead woman's scraps," Claire said.

"We all need to be on our watch to set the record straight," Greta declared. "You'll help, won't you, Alan?"

"Already working on it." Alan limped into the kitchen with his cane and some sheets of paper. "Hot cocoa, little one?"

While Alan made the cocoa at the stove with milk and sugar, Claire said goodbye to Granny Greta, who insisted she'd be fine to walk home on her own and didn't see the point of wasting money on a taxi. She left with another promise she'd set everyone she crossed straight if she heard so much as a hint of blame cast Claire's way. Claire felt sorry for anyone who crossed her Granny Greta. Her parting words were, "And remember, what Harris women lack in height, we make up for in spirit."

Her mother sloped off to run herself a bubble bath, and Claire joined her father at the back door. In one of his gardening coats, she followed him to the shed at the bottom of the garden. He carried the papers, and she took the mugs. Cream and marshmallows covered the surface, but she could smell the chocolate, which was already a step up from whatever machine-murdered swill Ramsbottom had served her.

While the portable heater did what it could to warm her father's tiny potting shed, Claire settled on the upturned plant pot in the corner. She'd once fit on it perfectly, though even with her knees almost hitting her chin, she'd keep perching on it until it cracked or she couldn't get back up anymore. Her father was reading whatever he'd printed off from the computer.

"Going over everything with Mum, I remembered some more things," Claire said. She took her first sip. Hot, sweet, and rich, and there might have been a splash of Bailey's. Only in December. "The assistant, Kirsty, said she was out clearing her head before she came back. Clearing her head from what? And when did she leave?"

"Good question," he said, still reading. "It would be a good idea to figure out *who* was in the house tonight and at *what* times. You said in the car the time of death was between five and five-thirty, and you didn't arrive until six forty-five, which means she was lying there for well over an hour. Why were you the first person to find her? Have you ever heard of Larry Evans?"

"Clue?"

"Artist." Alan sipped his hot chocolate, his nose hitting the cream. "Rather well respected, according to my research. What do you think?"

Alan held out a full-colour printout of a painting. At

first glance, it was a muddy mess of browns and reds in vaguely geometric shapes, but on closer inspection, Claire saw faces in the forms, and they all seemed to be screaming.

"It's like something from a nightmare," she said, unable to look away. "If you're wondering if Mum will let you hang one in the living room, I'd say it's a definite no."

"I came across Larry in my research. A critic described his work as 'Picasso after a weekend retreat in hell', and I'd say that's rather apt. Died two years ago, but his pieces still fetch large sums."

"I'm going to guess the surname isn't a coincidence?"

"Anne Evans, formerly Anne King, married Larry Evans five years before his death." He swapped the painting for a printout of Larry's obituary. "His only surviving heir was a daughter, so if she split everything with Anne, it explains her fortune."

"Worth killing for?"

"That's to be decided." After giving Claire a moment to read the obituary, Alan leaned back in his chair and asked, "What are you thinking, little one?"

"I'm thinking that I might have met his daughter, Bianca, already," she said, thinking back to the fair. "I was talking about Anne, and she said something. I can't remember what, exactly, but it wasn't good. Could have been a different Bianca."

"But it's another avenue to explore," he said. "You've

been around these people. Your foot is already in the door."

"Half of them probably think I did it."

"So, show them you didn't." Alan leaned forward, handing her the rest of his printed-out research. "Put the rumours to bed with the truth."

"Where do I even start?"

"Wherever your gut tells you to start."

"Starfall House," she said without needing to think about it. "I need to find out about this group of people who came with Anne. They all will have had access to Anne."

"Now you just need some motives."

"And here I thought we'd put the ghosts at that house to rest with Opal Jones."

"If anyone can bring peace to that house a second time, it's you." Alan raised his cup to her. "Now, let's get back in the house before we freeze. This cold snap can't come to an end soon enough."

And that wasn't the only thing.

Following her father back to the house as her mother's tasteful Christmas lights flashed around the window frames, Claire became all too aware of how excited she'd been for Christmas until things took a turn.

It was a Christmas of firsts for her.

Her first in the shop.

Her first with Ryan and the kids.

As much as she wanted a rest button, it didn't exist. Claire found herself wrapped in the middle of a web against her will. Could she wait around, hoping someone else would untangle it? Eugene, Greta, and the rest could try their best to defend her, but like her father said, Claire had to put the rumours to bed with the truth.

This was a web she had to untangle herself – and it had to be done before Christmas Day.

CHAPTER FIVE

*C*laire and Damon had predicted increased footfall over the three-day event. They'd even thrown around the idea opening the shop on Sunday for the first time to catch the stragglers. Damon had suggested they play it by ear. They'd had a taste of things on Friday, but by ten the following morning, the shop was the busiest Claire had seen it during the entire festive season.

Word of Anne's murder had spread throughout the village, but carloads of people had turned up with flyers for the Saturday fair anyway. After being turned away from the park by the police, the shoppers flooded into the village square, filling up every location that was vaguely artsy or crafty. Claire might not have been the only candle stall at the fair, but hers was definitely the only candle shop in Northash.

The busy shop was everything she'd wanted, yet it came with a catch. Half the people walking in had heard stories that led them to think Claire was behind Anne's death, and the other half heard about it once the whispers circled around.

"*I* heard she hit the woman's head with one of her candles until she looked like a puddle of jam," one woman whispered to Claire as she was stocking the central circular display with the first of the recently cured second batch of candy cane candles. "I wonder which scent it was."

"Definitely this one," Claire said, handing over a candle fresh from the box. "And you might want to buy a second because *I* heard she squashed the woman's head between two jars like she was crashing cymbals together."

Claire waited for the woman to cotton onto the obvious exaggeration, but like the other customers – none of whom were locals who knew Claire's identity – she gasped and let Claire pull her leg all the way out.

"*Cymbals?*" the woman said with a wicked smile, plucking out a second jar. "Can you imagine such a thing?"

The woman rushed straight to the counter, and Damon whizzed through the order in his usual efficient way. Claire finished restocking and lost another shred of hope in humanity.

"You should rebrand yourself as the Northash Ripper and get yourself accused of murder every week," Damon said when they paused for a coffee break during a lull. "And you were worried about the drama affecting our sales."

"I'd rather it not be at my expense. A few hundred years ago, they'd have me strapped in the dunking chair to see if I was a witch by now."

"Which is when candles would start falling miraculously from the sky to smite your enemies, which is how the story will end if *you* keep adding to it. Earlier, one woman said the candle exploded and blew Anne up like a land mine."

"I have to keep myself entertained, and as a considerate shopkeeper, I should give the people what they want, which is shocking scandal."

"And a souvenir of the murder weapon." Damon popped his head through to the shop. "I'll get back to serving. Don't you need to leave for lunch with Ryan?"

Claire glanced at the clock. An hour to go until she was due at Ryan's. She had been itching to get to Starfall House since first light. She hadn't expected to spend so much of the morning busy at the shop, spicing up the rumours.

"Will you be able to handle things on your own?"

"I scored eighty-nine million on *Dawn Ship 2* last night," he said, and if he had a collar, he'd have popped it. "I think I can handle one shop. Besides, I owe you. Eileen cancelled our dinner the second she heard about the murder. You saved me a night of torture."

Claire left through the back door. Rather than turning right to take the alley behind the row of shops to Christ Church Square to get to Ryan's early, Claire turned left and climbed the hill up to Starfall Park. Cars crowded every free space, swallowing the already narrow streets.

Beyond the unusually full Park Inn, the village's 'other pub', the police presence was evident at the park's front gates. People could still walk through, but officers were blocking the paths leading to the house. Claire hurried up the side street and through the trusty side entrance. With the morning ice melting, and without the trolley burden, she hopped over to the fountain, behind a white van, and onto the path running alongside the house. She saw familiar faces through the windows of the library, and it looked like they were having a meeting. Claire slipped past the two officers on duty outside the front door, busy throwing their sandwich crusts into the duck pond.

Officers were working on the other side of a cordon around the area where Claire had found Anne. They paid her no attention as they came and went up the stairs, so she approached the library. Lingering by the arch, Claire observed the meeting, seemingly led by Kirsty. She'd swapped the clipboard for a tablet and was pacing about. The only other two people in attendance were seated.

A slender man sat with long legs stretched out next to the short woman, who Claire knew to be Carol Poole, Anne's friend. Unless there were more men at the house, she assumed Mr Long Legs, somewhere in his fifties, was Scott, Anne's boyfriend. Of the three of them, he looked the most distant from Kirsty's barely audible rambling.

"If The Park Inn is letting people put up stalls, why don't we join them?" Carol suggested. Claire's ears tuned into their quiet talking with nothing else to pick up on; the officers were working mutely. "I'm sure they'll have room for us."

"We have room here," Kirsty insisted, sighing as though exhausted by having to explain herself. "We have the perfect space for this kind of craft fair. All we have to do is postpone and rearrange. There's still time to pull everything together before Christmas. Why should we have to compromise?"

"Why compromise?" Carol's voice suddenly rose. "Anne is dead, Kirsty. My friend. Scott's girlfriend. Look at the poor man. He's torn up."

Scott's legs twitched at the mention of his name, and he snapped back from whatever faraway place his mind had been visiting. He looked straight at Claire. He gave her away with a clearing of his throat.

"You," Kirsty said.

Claire remembered Anne saying something similar at the fair, though Kirsty didn't have the same anger and didn't lift her finger to point at her again. Claire had hoped Mark would be present in case she needed someone on her side, but she'd heard a shred of an apology in Kirsty's single world. Maybe this wouldn't be such an uphill battle.

"The police confirmed that I was in my shop when Anne was murdered," Claire announced, approaching them in the middle of the room. "Between five and five-thirty."

"Yes, which I've already told them is impossible," Kirsty said, back to sounding annoyed. "Because I didn't leave until six. I walked right down those stairs and she wasn't there. They must have got it wrong."

Or her body was moved.

Claire thought back to the scene. It seemed so obvious now. She hadn't noticed any blood around Anne, only around her candle. Rather than challenging Kirsty with the idea, she decided it would be better to play along.

"Well, whatever happened, I've officially been ruled out," Claire said, taking a chair. "I'm interested in clearing my name and discovering what really happened to Anne. I know Em, the owner, and she told me Anne was hoping to buy the house. Is that right, Carol? You were the one who told her about this place."

"Yes, I did," Carol said, her defences shooting straight up with a stiffening of her spine. "Anne had been trying to find somewhere in Oxfordshire or the surrounding area, but it didn't matter how much of a fortune Larry left her. Money always stretches further up north. Anne said this was the perfect place for The Collective's headquarters."

"The Collective?" Claire asked as Kirsty pulled up another chair and joined them; Claire must have taken hers. "Sounds mysterious."

"It's us," Kirsty said. "It was all Anne's idea. She envisioned a communal base where creatives could live and make art. We're all artists, and for one reason or another, we thought it would be a good idea to follow Anne up here to give her concept a go."

"My husband died a few years ago," Carol said, scratching at her neck, her tone still defensive. "Thought it would give me more time to sculpt, which is all I want to do now. I have so much built-up emotion, I need to create, and I can't stand another night in that bed and breakfast separated from my art. I need to find out if we're allowed into our rooms yet."

Carol tore herself away from the chair and left the library.

"We're all taking things differently," Scott said,

pushing himself up. He loomed over Claire, offering his hand. He gave Kirsty a run in the height department. "Scott Harper. I'd be happy to help in any way I can, but not at this moment. Like Carol said, the bed and breakfast wasn't the best place to be last night, and none of us got much sleep. Excuse me, but I'd also like to get up to my room. I can't imagine how much longer they can spend in there."

Scott bowed out of the room, leaving Kirsty and Claire alone. Kirsty had taken to tapping on the tablet. It looked like she was typing an email. She was eager to get on with her work, yet it hadn't been twenty-four hours since her boss died. What had Mark said about Kirsty insinuating she'd done all the work planning the fair?

"It must take a lot to plan a fair," Claire said, as friendly as she could muster toward the woman who'd been screaming that she was a murderer only the previous day. "I run a shop, and that's hard enough. With as many stalls as you have here and all the people you were expecting, I can't imagine it was easy to pull off."

"It's what I'm good at," she said with a shrug. "I put a lot of work into pulling everything together. I'm determined to see the full vision come to life." She paused her tapping and added, like an afterthought, "Anne would have wanted to see it succeed. The fair was her idea, after all."

"But you planned it all?"

"That's why I'm here."

"As her assistant," Claire confirmed. "So, unlike everyone else in The Collective, you're not here for the art. You're here to fulfil a specific role. If your boss is dead, why continue with the fair?"

"Because I invested a lot of time in it. It's not like I was being paid. I'm doing it for the love of it."

"You work for free?"

"In exchange for my living expenses here," Kirsty said with a nod, as though nothing about this was unusual. "And you're wrong. I'm here for the art as much as everyone else. I think The Collective is a brilliant idea, but it's just that, an idea. There's no paperwork. There's nothing official. If Anne's not here to carry on, why shouldn't I?"

"So, you want to step into the role of leader of The Collective?" Claire asked, feeling like she had to catch up with where Kirsty's head was. "And stay in this house? How can you afford it?"

"That's where the fair comes in," Kirsty said, taking in the expanse of the library. "Who's to say it has to be a one-off? This building already has permission to be a mixed-use commercial space. If the market succeeds, we can keep renting off Em to see what The Collective could grow into."

Claire felt an opportunity to get one back on Kirsty with a finger-pointed accusation. She'd just served up the perfect motive for murder on a platter, but Claire wasn't there to score points.

"You were walking around the park before you came back and found Anne," Claire said, changing course. "Out clearing your head."

"Yes." Kirsty's matter-of-fact tone was betrayed by the hesitation as her fingers paused tapping for the first time. "I was out for forty-five minutes."

"Hardly the warmest weather for a forty-five-minute walk after dark."

"I wrapped up quite warm, I assure you." Kirsty locked the tablet and dropped it into a bag. "I've become quite taken with the Chinese garden. I find myself there most nights. Ask anyone."

"But did anyone see you on your walk?"

"Not that I know of." Kirsty shook her head. "You're digging in the wrong patch if you think I did it. I respected Anne. We had a great working relationship, and that's all I have to say about it. Now, if you'll excuse me, I need to go and see what's going on at The Park Inn. If they've poached my stallholders, I hope they've put some money aside for our commission."

"Before you go … if not you, then who?"

"I'm sorry?"

"Which of The Collective?" Claire joined her in standing. "If it was neither me or you, it must have crossed your mind that the murderer must be one of the group."

"Yes, it had." Kirsty slung the bag over her shoulder, eyes on the archway. She paused and said, "Mark was the last person she expected to follow her up here. Of all the members in The Collective, Mark made her life here the most difficult."

"How so?"

"He treated his mother like she didn't possess a brain," she said flatly. "And he'll probably make some sarcastic comment along the lines of 'course Kirsty accused me', but it's what I think. Ever since she came into that money, he's been hounding her about her will."

"Do you know when she last updated it?"

"She didn't tell me everything."

With that, Kirsty left the library. Claire lingered for a moment longer, glancing at the corner she'd been stuck in. Maybe she was there in an alternate universe, having the best time of her life, already friends with Anne after bonding over their love of candles. She should have pressed Kirsty about being rejected initially, not that she was sure it mattered anymore.

Claire wasn't selling candles in this universe, but she was at the crime scene, and half the suspects were on her doorstep. With half an hour until she was due at Ryan's, she'd be a fool not to talk to someone else.

After what Kirsty said about Mark, Claire most wanted to talk to him, though as she left the library for the main entrance, she wouldn't have minded talking to Kirsty again. She'd dodged the question about what had driven her into the park to clear her head, suggesting it was routine.

"I had a feeling I'd find you snooping about here sooner or later," DI Ramsbottom said, approaching from the archway to the sitting room. "Cracked the case yet?"

"I wish I could say I have."

"As do I." Ramsbottom reached into his pocket and pulled out a packet of the familiar Merry Crispmas crisps from The Hesketh Arms. He unravelled the top and plucked out a small handful before offering them to Claire. "I think it's turkey and stuffing myself."

"It's never that simple," Claire said, taking a bite of the crisp that tasted like all of Christmas and yet nothing specific. "There's definitely cranberry in there."

"Ah, yes, I can taste that now," Ramsbottom said, returning for another handful. Claire declined more. "I'm not long off the phone with your father. Has he told you the good news?"

"No?"

"You've been further expunged from involvement in Anne's murder. The damage to the candle doesn't match the wound on Anne's head. Early tests suggest the heel of a shoe was behind the impact on the candle, and Anne wasn't killed with a glass object. Nor a cylinder. She was struck with something flatter. We're still trying to figure out what, exactly."

"The blood?"

"It was Anne's. They must have added it to the candle."

"The blood on the tiles," Claire corrected. "It was smeared rather than pooled. And there was hardly any blood around Anne. Kirsty said her body wasn't there when she left at six. The way Anne was lying struck me as odd. Still, and staring up. The more I think about it, the more it looks like she was placed there rather than landing after being hit over the head. Was she killed somewhere else and moved?"

"Crikey, Claire, you don't miss a beat," Ramsbottom said, glancing around as he drew Claire further into the corner. "We've been combing the entire house, opening rooms to the guests as they're ruled out. We believe Anne was murdered in her own room and then transported, very cleanly and neatly, to the foot of the stairs."

"And my candle was the cherry on the top."

"A last-ditch attempt to throw off the scent," he said, tapping his nose, "if you'll pardon the pun. And if you'll pardon me. I have some more enquiries to make. All top secret, of course, but keep me informed if you discover anything, won't you, Claire?"

"One more thing, Detective," Claire said, fumbling for a question. She still wanted to talk to someone else, and the DI would know who was in which room. "Which room is Carol in?"

"That one just there, next to the bathroom," he said. "Good luck. She's rather upset."

———

CLAIRE WASN'T SURE SHE'D EVER SEEN SOMEONE SCULPT IN real life. She was positive she'd never seen someone sculpting while shedding streams of tears. Some were making their way to the clay, but Carol Poole worked them into the twisted creation with her thickly coated fingers.

Her hands worked the clay in a way that looked instinctive, never pausing to make decisions. Similar distorted designs decorated the surfaces in her otherwise stark room, which was so neutral that only the sculptures drew attention. A living space, studio, and museum all in one.

"She was my best friend," Carol spoke through the tears, tilting her head as she pulled out the clay at a new angle. "Like a sister, really. Pull up a pillow. But before you do that, can you grab me that cardigan? The air's taken on a bite."

Claire picked up a red cardigan hanging on the back of the door and kicked over a scatter cushion from a pile. Everything in Carol's room was low to the ground, including her futon bed. Even her clay moulding was done cross-legged on the floor.

"You're going to have to hold open the arms for me," she said, holding out her terracotta fingers like a statue come to life. "I can't break the flow."

Claire scrunched up the cardigan's sleeves and Carol carefully guided her hands through. For all her crying, her hand was as steady as stone. The cardigan, which hadn't seemed so big when Claire picked it up, draped behind Carol like a cape.

"Thank you." Carol resumed her moulding, though the crying had stopped. "We were both estate agents. I enjoyed it for a time, but I knew I wanted out when my Ronnie died. He was a sculptor. Well, he was more of a welder, but he welded these great metal creations. Spent half his life chasing the dream of making himself famous with those things. Died from a heart attack atop a ladder. Maybe the heart attack wouldn't have killed him, but combined with the fall, he didn't stand a chance." Still no tears. Her elfin face had taken on a flat, sombre expression. "He was the sort of man who always wanted the dinner on the table at a certain time and his shirts ironed a specific way. It took him dying for me to realise I'd been living in servitude to the man, as my mother did my father. It must have been servitude because I felt completely liberated. Not right away, but soon enough I realised I could do anything and be anyone. It was quite simple. I wanted to move my body and make things with my hands."

"So, you stopped working as an estate agent when your husband died?"

"Well, no," Carol said with a shake of her head. "I kept working. My awakening was a slow one. There was a period where I had to grieve for the woman I was and the woman I never became. When Anne's Larry died of a heart attack, like Ronnie, it brought us closer together. She told me about her idea for The Collective, and I thought it was brilliant. I sold my house and came along to do those two things. I get to spend all day making sculptures, and with Northash being semi-rural, there's a walking trail in every direction. Until I saw Anne in the hallway yesterday, our short time here was the happiest of my life."

Claire believed her pain, but she also immediately picked up on something else.

"You arrived after her body was discovered," Claire said. "So, you never saw her in the hallway."

"Yes, I did," Carol affirmed, frowning at Claire. "I insisted upon it. They left her there on the cold floor so they could prod and poke and gather evidence, but I needed to see her with my own eyes. Seeing the ones we love after they've passed helps heal the soul so it can accept what has happened."

Claire couldn't argue with that. Seeing her

grandfathers in their coffins had helped with the grieving somewhat. She wasn't sure how much that applied to seeing someone at a murder scene. The image of Anne had certainly stuck with Claire in a way she couldn't shake, but she couldn't claim to be anything close to a friend of Anne's. Perhaps Carol had thought quick on her feet to explain having seen the body after striking Anne? Given how many people had been at the crime scene, it wouldn't be too difficult to check.

"Where were you returning from?" Claire said.

"A hike." Carol's fingers worked, but her eyes were firmly fixed on Claire. "I crossed the canal and took the trail through the forest up to the factory. Looped past the allotments and came out at the top of the park."

"That's quite a walk. You must have been out all day?"

"Like I said, I like to move my body." Carol stretched her arms above her head. "Do you have many more questions? I'm finding it hard to create authentic art with your gaze upon me. My emotions are too raw. I've just lost a friend. A sister."

Claire heard a hint of a correction in Carol's voice as she again upgraded 'friend' to 'sister.'

"I am sorry for your loss," Claire said, sensing that her time in the sculptor's studio was ending. After Carol had initially yelled at her for daring to knock on her door during her 'process', Claire was surprised she'd spoken to her at all. "I wanted to speak to you above the others because I wanted to talk to someone who knew Anne. A son, a boyfriend, an assistant, they're all going to see a different side than a friend."

"Yes, I'd agree with that," Carol said, her smile fond. "We confided a great deal in each other, especially after bonding over being widows. We drifted a little after she retired from work."

"Was that five years ago when she met Larry Evans?" Claire asked, remembering the article her father had attached. "They met at an art gallery?"

"Anne was a keen admirer of art. She'd never heard of Larry, but he just happened to be standing next to her in the gallery when she was taking in one of his paintings. He asked her what she thought. His idea of a joke. He had that sort of sense of humour. Anne being Anne, she gave her honest opinion. She told him it was grim and morbid, and whoever painted it must be deeply troubled, but she couldn't deny that it was intriguing. I can still see the moment he fell in love with her. It was like something from a film. They married quickly after. Maybe we hadn't heard of Larry Evans, but enough people had because the guy was filthy rich. We'd both talked about retiring for years. I was so jealous of her going off to live a life of luxury in his manor house." Carol paused, tore a chunk of the sculpture clean off, and began reworking the nub. "I was happy for her, of course. Who wouldn't be? She'd invite me out sometimes. It was after Larry died of that heart attack that we really bonded again. We've been close ever since." Carol paused, her brows dropping in a look of complete sadness. "We *were* close. Just for a moment, I think I forgot what had happened. Oh, Anne. What happened to you?"

Carol's tears started afresh, her hands working the clay harder with each press. Claire sensed that if she stayed much longer, the sculpture would be worked down to nothing.

"The police think Anne was killed in her bedroom and then moved to where she was found, which suggests that someone in The Collective was behind Anne's death. You all live together. You must see and hear things. Who do you think did it?"

Carol looked around the room as though she'd just been asked an illicit question or feared someone might hear her response. To Claire's surprise, she paused her sculpting and seemed to think about it.

"Mark seemed to be causing her an awful lot of aggravation," Carol said. "Anne thought his behaviour toward her changed when she inherited all she did from Larry. The house, his fortune, his paintings, his art collection. Mark became obsessed with what she was going to do with it all. I don't think she liked that he followed her up here. Some boys just never know when to let go of their mothers. It's not like she was on her own. She had Scott."

"Do you know when they met?"

"We'd just moved up here," she said. "They had a chance meeting in the pub. I think it was love at first sight. Anne was lucky to have found love for a third time. I don't think she fully appreciated what she had with Scott."

Carol's mouth opened as if to continue talking, but she didn't continue her train of thoughts. She placed her hands on the clay, unmoving, as though hearing the echo of what she'd just said. Claire had heard a tinge of jealousy in Carol's voice – not for the first time since the start of their conversation.

"What was their relationship like?"

"You'll have to talk to Scott about that," she said, her voice shrinking as her focus returned to her sculpture. "I really would like to be left alone now."

Claire pushed herself off the carpet and tossed the pillow back onto the pile while taking in the row of sculptures on a shelf. If Anne thought Larry's paintings were morbid, Claire wondered what she had thought of Carol's twisted creations. There was nothing inherently human about them, yet their forms contorted like collections of broken limbs, Carol's hand-working visible over every inch of the clay.

Each statue had a large, flat base. If one of Carol's sculptures had killed Anne, the clay would show up in the tests. Something to consider. For now, Claire wasn't sure.

Carol had given her a lot to think about and had pointed another finger at Mark. He was starting to look less and less like the jolly guy who'd saved her from icy doom only yesterday morning.

She wanted to talk to him as soon as possible.

And Scott, the boyfriend.

And Kirsty, for that matter.

But first, lunch at Ryan's.

CHAPTER SIX

*I*n the cellar under Ryan's terraced house in Christ Church Square, Claire watched as Ryan delicately dipped the pointed tip of his brush into a cup of swampy water. He tickled the wet nib against a palette covered in so much paint that it looked like he'd never cleaned it, but the shade he cooked up blended in perfectly with the wash of blue on the canvas. Like when Claire mixed up scents for new candles, Ryan seemed to rely on his creative instincts.

And doing a fantastic job of it. She wasn't sure how far along Ryan was into the painting, but she could already see an accurate semblance of the reference picture on his phone. A set of steep tiled steps wound down a dense street of houses and shops. A few people were dotted around, their lack of shorts and t-shirts the only hint of the winter weather. The sky and ocean were so tranquil past the white buildings with terracotta roofs it might as well have been taken in the height of summer. The image couldn't have been further from current weather in Northash. Beyond the stomping of Amelia and Hugo as they ran around upstairs, Claire was sure she could hear the patter of rain.

"It's looking great," she said quietly, not wanting to disturb him. Ryan rarely painted in front of her, but he'd picked up his brush when she'd followed him down to his studio. "I'm surprised you wanted to come back when you could be standing there staring at the ocean all day."

"Northash has its own kind of beauty," he said, gesturing to the wall of paintings depicting the local lush green countryside on warmer days. "Besides, this place has more for me than a scenic view to paint." He smiled at Claire over his shoulder, causing her stomach to do that thing only Ryan could make it do. "With all the years I spent there, I thought I'd feel like I was going home, yet I spent most of the two weeks homesick for this place. The kids were the same. They kept asking when we could come back, and they were born there."

"What is it they say? Home is where the heart is." Sipping the coffee Ryan had given her on arrival, Claire took in a few sunny Spain paintings on a nearby table. "And where the art is. You haven't wasted any time."

"They felt urgent. I didn't pick up a paintbrush all the

time I lived there, which is funny because it's the one thing I probably should have done. Em calls it 'art therapy', and I don't think she's far off. Could have helped all those years."

Ryan's brush hesitated over the canvas. Given how finished the other paintings seemed, he'd spent every second since coming home painting. Had he been working through the disappointment of not finding Maya? Claire wanted to ask, but questions about Maya never rolled off her tongue, nor did answers come easily for Ryan. He opened up in whispers rather than shouts, and Claire resisted the urge to scream every question she had about his two weeks away from the top of her lungs.

Ryan's arms slipped around her middle from behind, pulling her from the paintings and her thoughts. "You know, I could only think about seeing you for the twenty minutes between getting off the plane and turning my phone on. That wait for you to get out of the police station felt like a lifetime."

"I wish that's how things had gone. And it dragged out for me too. I've had a head full of Mariah Carey lyrics echoing in the back of my head ever since. And all for nothing. I'm happy to report that Ramsbottom has 'expunged' me from the case. Turns out it wasn't even a candle that killed her. The scene I stumbled upon was as staged as a Nativity play."

Ryan's arms pulled away. "Someone tried to frame you?"

"Looks that way."

"You seem awfully calm about that."

"I don't think it was personal," she said. "Well, as 'not personal' as being framed for murder gets. Whoever killed her saw what happened at the fair and faked clues to start the police off on the wrong foot."

Claire paused, wondering if there was a way for the police to identify what kind of shoe had stomped on her candle. Surely that information would narrow things down. She made a mental note to ask Ramsbottom the next time she saw him.

"Maybe it's the DI's daughter in me, but *knowing* I *am* innocent is enough. I do have *some* trust in the police, although Ramsbottom seems in over his toupee, as per usual."

Ryan laughed, abandoning his paintbrush in the cup of water. Claire almost wished Anne's murder hadn't come up. Each new trickle of information from Ryan gave Claire the feeling his years abroad had been far from the sunny day he'd spent his morning painting.

"I'm surprised this is connected to Larry Evans," Ryan said, flicking through the printouts Claire had brought with her as she followed him up the stairs. "His work feels so familiar."

"And creepy."

"I'm sure my mum had something of his in the house when I was a kid." He stared off for a moment. "Are they worth a lot?"

"Do you mean are they worth killing for?" Claire considered her response as they came up into the dining area. She'd been right about the rain. The sun had half slipped away already. "Undecided. I don't know if they factor in at all, but Carol said Anne inherited them. I wonder where they are."

"*Daaad?*" Amelia called from the living room. "We're hungry."

"You said we were having lunch," Hugo added.

"I'm a little light on supplies." Ryan consulted the fridge before moving onto the cupboard. "We can have baked beans with … tinned potatoes and cheese. How about something from the chippy?"

"And here I was expecting the usual grilled chicken and salad."

"We're celebrating," he said, kissing her. "I really did miss you, Claire. I don't know how we didn't see each other all that time. It feels like such a waste."

"We're here now. I have my shoes on, so lunch is on me, and I can check on the shop. Might be able to sneak away for the rest of the day if it's quiet."

"Yeah?" A cheeky smile produced his dimples. "Em offered to watch the kids again tonight. Maybe I should take her up on it?"

"Maybe you should." Claire accepted a kiss on her neck before pulling away as Ryan's hands wrapped around her waist. "Chips first. Curry sauce or gravy?"

"Both."

"Now you're just being greedy. Get some plates warming in the oven. I shouldn't be long."

Leaving Ryan in the kitchen, Claire hurried into the hallway. She glanced at the basket of umbrellas, but the whistling wind behind the door would have her going from nought to Mary Poppins in no time. Shrugging off her jacket, she swapped it for one of Ryan's waterproof coats. Once upon a time, she'd been able to fit into his clothes, but she wasn't going to attempt to zip it up after squeezing her arms in. A glance in the mirror as she tipped the fur-lined hood over her hair reminded her of the OJ Simpson trial she'd seen on the TV as a kid. What had they said about the glove not fitting?

Amelia appeared in the doorway. "Come look at our pictures."

"We put them in a photo album," Hugo said from behind her, holding up a book. "Like you used to in the old days."

Claire saw her age reflected in the young children's eyes as they stared expectantly at her. They still held the glimmer of excitement from when she'd arrived and they'd first run up to her in the hallway. They'd greeted her with tight hugs, which had made her realise Ryan wasn't the only one she'd missed.

"Show me over lunch," Claire said, already on her way to the door. "Won't be long!"

Head down against the bitter combination of icy rain and a cheek-stinging gale, Claire hurried around the corner to the main square. She glanced through the shop window and found the place back to its usual wintery quietness. She popped her head through the door, and given the way Damon jumped from behind his laptop at the counter, she guessed he was trying to beat last night's score of eighty-nine million.

"Take it," Damon said when she asked about the rest of the day. "Rain scared off the craft fair crowd, and I can't imagine many more will come. I heard it was going to snow. I'll lock up – on one condition." He closed the laptop and stretched out. "Grab me a chip teacake from next door. It's nice and warm here. Speaking of which…"

Getting the hint, Claire backed out of the shop and hopped into The Abbey Fryer fish and chip shop next door, which was empty thanks to the rain. Claire ordered two large portions of chips, battered fish, a couple of jumbo sausages, gravy and curry, and Damon's chip teacake. Leaning against the shiny silver counter, she investigated the glowing warming box. She wondered if she had room for a potato pie too.

The door behind her opened, letting in the cold wind along with Mark's familiar voice.

"I *know* you know," she heard him growl in the imitation of a whisper. "I know what your game is."

Claire almost turned, but the bite in Mark's voice kept her staring ahead. She recoiled into the hood while the young woman behind the counter shook salt over a portion of chips fresh from the fryer.

"Well?" Mark pushed. "You can't avoid me forever."

Claire averted her eyes from the pie to the shiny silver frame. The other man's voice was familiar and more local than Mark's. She could make out Mark's flat cap, and from his companion's slender height, Scott was the man he'd growled at.

"My girlfriend – your mother – died *yesterday*," Scott said measuredly, making Mark's tone seem all the darker. "I'm *grieving*, as is everyone else, which is why I'm here to get lunch for them."

"Always playing the big man."

"Some of us aren't playing." Despite the venom in Mark's voice, Scott didn't stoop to join him by adding any of his own. "You've spent the last twenty-four hours digging for your mother's will. What does that say about you?"

"That I cared about her."

"About her money, more like."

"Coming from you?" Mark sounded dumbfounded. "*You* have it, don't you?"

"I've already told you. I don't even know if she had one. We didn't talk about it. If you don't mind, I haven't eaten since yesterday, and neither has half the house. Make yourself useful for once and leave me alone."

A silence stretched out for a moment before the door opened again. Claire watched Mark's blurry figure leave the chippy. He slammed the door, rattling the letter box and silencing the place to the low hum of the radio.

"What can I get you?" the young woman asked with an exasperated sigh as she placed Claire's paper-wrapped items into a white plastic bag.

"Three large portions of chips," Scott said, joining Claire at the counter. He glanced in her direction and offered a tight smile, as one did when close to a stranger, but his gaze didn't linger on the face buried under the hood's fur lining. He plucked a menu from a stand on the counter and opened it, more interested in rubbing the corner than reading the contents. "What paper stock is this?"

"Come again?" the girl behind the counter asked, passing Claire a plastic bag fit to bursting. "Anything else, love?"

Claire shook her head and turned to leave, making sure to face away from Scott on her way to the door. She'd been in the right place and time to hear Mark's outburst. Now that she knew Mark was interested in tracking down his mother's will, she was interested in putting her thoughts to him. Given Carol and Kirsty's accusations, Claire was starting to see a different picture of Mark than the one she'd first formed after meeting him on the ice.

"Making healthy choices, I hope!" Em said, on her way to the gym in rainbow layers, with a yoga mat tucked under her arm.

"It's mostly a bag of vegetables," Claire replied, returning Em's wave, "in the form of potatoes. Though they are deep-fat fried. I ordered enough for a small army. Join us for lunch at Ryan's?"

"I have zucchini noodles and a yoga class waiting for me." Em hesitated by the gym as the doors slid open. "But you enjoy your celebration. And tell Ryan I got his message and I'd love to babysit tonight. See you later!"

Leaving Em to light up the gym, Claire turned the corner toward Christ Church Square. So deep in thought when she'd left the chippy, she hadn't noticed that the rain had stopped. As much as she wanted to go over the questions she wanted to ask Mark, having the day to spend with Ryan excited her too much to give it any thought.

Her footsteps splashed through the puddles that had settled in the cobbles. She'd waited two weeks for a slice of the ordinary with Ryan and the kids. Starfall House and what happened to Anne Evans could wait until morning.

"I come bringing carbohydrates," Claire called down the hallway as she let herself in with her key. "I hope you're all hungry. I might have ordered a little too—"

A door slammed upstairs, cutting Claire off; she could hardly believe she was walking into the same house she'd left only minutes earlier. Tugging her key from the door, she wiped her feet on the mat and looked down the hallway to Ryan. He was clutching the sink, his head bowed. Hugo was sniffling in the sitting room, curled up in an armchair.

"I wasn't gone that long," Claire said as she approached the kitchen. "Feels like a bomb went off in—"

Ryan glanced over his shoulder with red eyes as she walked in. Claire went to put the chippy bag on the counter so she could comfort him over whatever had happened, but she didn't get there. Her head whipped to the dining table. They weren't alone. A woman with cascading dark hair and a made-up face was sitting at the kitchen table, and Claire knew who she was right away.

"Who is this?" the woman asked Ryan, though her eyes were on Claire. "*This* is *her?*"

Ryan's hand slipped around Claire's. He clenched it

for dear life, but Claire couldn't take her eyes away from the newcomer as she rose from the table. She wore tight-fitting athletic wear that hugged every perfectly rounded curve of her body, and she was staring at Claire as though she was a stray cat who had gone through the wrong cat flap.

"Maya, this is Claire," Ryan said, finding his voice. "My girlfriend. Claire, this is—"

"His wife," Maya interrupted, a brow arching slowly as she scanned Claire from foot to face. She followed it up with something spoken swiftly in Spanish – something Ryan did as rarely as he let her watch him paint.

In the tense silence that followed, Claire longed to be back in that moment. She didn't need to speak the language to understand what had been said. Like Mark in the chippy, Ryan's defensive tone filled in the gaps, and she was sure Maya had insulted her.

"Hugo." Maya's eyes left Claire for the first time since she entered the room and flicked to the doorway. A smile lit up her face, the contrast highlighting how much her upper lip had risen into a sneer. She spoke in Spanish, and Hugo darted into the kitchen. He'd recently turned eight, but he was small for his age and had the presence of a child half his age as he snuck behind the safety of Claire and Ryan. One of his hands clung to the back of the coat Claire still wore.

She'd only gone out for chips.

"Hugo, why don't you go and check on Amelia?" Ryan sent Hugo on his way with a kiss on the forehead. While Hugo padded up the stairs, Ryan closed the door and returned to the sink, keeping the dining table between them and Maya. Claire could have heard a candle crackle in the dead silence.

"You can't waltz in expecting everything to be okay," Ryan said firmly, an arm outstretched, his fingers spread. "You left them."

Maya sank back into the chair, though in an unhurried way. The accusation barely seemed to scrape the edges. Settled, she went back to staring at Claire as though the stray cat had started scratching the wallpaper.

"Not with her here," she said bluntly. "Please, leave us alone."

"Claire isn't going anywhere, Maya. You don't get to dictate these things. I spent two weeks looking for you."

"Why do you think I'm here?" Maya motioned to her suitcase. "You visited almost every member of my family to find out where I was. I'm right here. You must have wanted to talk to me, and I will not talk with her here."

As much as Claire wanted to chime in, she knew it wasn't the time or place to add to an already tense situation. Swallowing the lump in her throat, Claire looped her hand around Ryan's and pulled him into the hallway. Two sets of knees poked out around the curve of the staircase. Claire took a deep breath, summoning every ounce of maturity she'd gained over her years stumbling through adulthood.

"I know you don't want to do this alone," she said, "and I wish I could be here, but I think I'm only going to get in the way of you two having the conversations you need to have. I think you know it too."

Ryan offered a nod and let go of Claire's hand. "I wish you weren't, but I think you're right. I just wish she wasn't here like this. And now."

"Well, she is." Claire pulled him into a hug. She saw Maya watching them through the gap in the door. "I'll only be around the corner."

The cold winter air was refreshing after how suffocating the house had felt. Claire hurried back to the shop, still wearing Ryan's coat, and dumped the bag from the chippy on the counter. She'd lost awareness of clinging onto it sometime around entering Ryan's house.

"I thought you'd done a runner with my teacake," Damon called from the back of the shop as a teaspoon rattled around a cup. "Coffee?"

"Sure." Alone in the shop, Claire leaned against the counter and pushed against it like Ryan had held himself upright at the sink. She took a few deep breaths before snapping up as Damon walked in. "Change of plans. I'm sticking around."

"Everything alright?"

"Yep." Claire started unloading the bag. "And lucky for

us, we've got half the chippy stock to get us through the day."

"Crikey, Claire. More like the next week. Do you have dibs on anything?"

"No." Claire sank into the chair behind the counter. "What were you telling me about that *Dawn Ship* high score earlier?"

"Oh, yeah," Damon muttered through a mouthful of jumbo sausage, half wrapped in the greasy paper. "So, you have a base score of two hundred thousand, and then you get fifty per squadron run, but only if you're in elite mode, which you *should* be if you've been playing for as long as *I* have. So, anyway, Sean was captain and we…"

Staring ahead as she picked at the chips Damon had dumped in front of her, Claire tuned out. Not just of Damon, but the shop, and maybe even the whole of Northash. In all her years of friendship with Damon, from the candle factory to the shop, she wasn't sure she'd ever tried to hide her emotions from him. She just couldn't bring herself to say out loud what had happened – not that she'd be able to escape it for long.

Maya was in Northash, and Claire had never felt smaller than she had beneath the gaze of – as Maya had reminded Claire – her boyfriend's wife.

.

CHAPTER SEVEN

*C*leaning up the morning after the night before usually included more than plucking chamomile teabags from mugs. If Sally hadn't been busy with her children and Damon at the Trafford Centre, Claire might have awoken with the dreaded red wine fog clouding her brain.

"Not only is Damon enjoying himself," Sally had said as the sound of the busy shopping mall echoed around her the previous night, "but I think my kids like him more than me. Could never get Paul to do something like this. The words 'Christmas shopping at the Trafford Centre on a Saturday night' would have been Paul's worst nightmare. Everything alright, mate?"

"Just wanted to catch up," Claire lied. "Talk about

what happened at Starfall. I heard you had contact with Anne Evans."

Sally dealt more with Kirsty, who she'd judged to be 'a bit bossy', which was as far as Claire let the conversation go. Her current situation would have been the pin to pop Sally's bubble.

Claire bumped into Em on the way back from the shop. Suitably filled in after an earlier brief conversation with Ryan at the gym, where he tried to extend his holiday leave, Em followed Claire back to her flat.

After pouring her heart out and concluding that Ryan needed space and support, they sipped chamomile tea instead of wine. Claire ate Cadbury's Dairy Milk from the shop while Em grinned her way through a 90% coco bar, which was so bitter Claire couldn't understand how it could be classified as chocolate. Em sent Claire off to her room for an early night, and she awoke the following day glad to have someone as responsible as Em in her life.

Claire jabbed the coffee machine button. Though she felt well rested, she hadn't felt well rested enough to forgo her morning coffee since her teens.

"Sorry if the water pressure wasn't great," Claire said as Em made her way across the flat to the spare bedroom. "Been meaning to have it looked at."

"Compared to the shower on my narrowboat, it's absolutely divine." Em ran her towel over her head. She'd let her usual buzzcut grow into a prickly half an inch.

"Thank you for letting me spend the night. I missed the water rocking last night, but it was lovely to be somewhere with central heating this time of year."

"It was a cold one last night." Claire took her first sip of the day and almost scalded her mouth. "You're welcome here any time. You know that."

"And what a fine job you've done of making it your own," Em said as she shook out the duvet. "I noticed the drawers were filled with the children's things. I just want to say I really think it's great how you've welcomed them into your life as you have. They seem to have really bonded with you."

"Always thought I was rubbish with kids. I could never seem to get Sally's two on my side, but it's different with Amelia and Hugo. Maybe it's because they're Ryan's, but I feel protective of them." Claire stared off in the direction of Ryan's house and felt a pang in her chest. "I wonder how they're taking all of this. They were both so upset yesterday. I've never seen them like that. I should have gone upstairs to check on them before I left, but I wanted to leave as much as Maya wanted me out of there."

"Fight, flight, freeze, and your body chose flight." Em rested a hand on Claire's shoulder. "Don't beat yourself up for being human. They all know you care about them, and you'll be there for them when the moment is right. These things have a way of sorting themselves out. If I'm not mistaken, that white glow around the curtains can only mean one thing."

Em walked past Claire and hopped over Domino, currently lying in her favourite spot where the radiator pipes could be felt through the carpet in front of the TV. Em pulled back the curtains to a blinding blanket of white.

"Damon was right." Claire sipped her cooling coffee. "It snowed."

Claire joined Em at the window, where Sid was already on the windowsill taking in the view. A fresh blanket of fluffy snow had covered the square, making the clock tower look even more like something plucked from a postcard than usual. Thank goodness it was Sunday and the shop wasn't open; nobody would venture out shopping in this, and the gritters had been nowhere near the place.

"I could stand here all day looking at this," Em said, letting out a contented sigh, "but alas, the real world knocks. I need to get to Starfall House. Kirsty has set up a meeting. I think she wants to discuss what happens with the house now that Anne is no longer in the picture. After what you told me last night about Kirsty wanting to continue The Collective, I think it's best if we're all on the same page."

"Mind if I tag along?"

"I assumed you would," Em said, pulling herself away

from the window after a tickle of Sid's head. "I asked everyone from The Collective to be there for the meeting, so it will be the perfect opportunity for you to ask about this candle situation. It doesn't sit right with me that one of them would try to frame you."

"WE'RE NOT HERE TO DISCUSS *THAT*," KIRSTY SAID brusquely, striding into the library at Starfall House. "This meeting is about the future of The Collective, not what happened to Anne."

"What happened to my mother affects the future of The Collective," Mark said, sending Claire a smile. She couldn't return it after how she'd overheard him acting in the chippy yesterday. "We're all subject of this police investigation whether we like it or not."

"Claire has been dragged into it through no fault of her own, and she deserves answers," Em said. "So, does anyone know how one of her candles ended up at the foot of the stairs covered in blood with a boot print on it?"

Claire looked around the room. Just as they'd done when Em first asked the question, they looked at each other as though waiting for someone else to say something. Carol pulled her red cardigan around herself and tapped her foot, no doubt counting down the minutes until she could get back to crying into her clay. Scott's long legs fidgeted as he looked around, and Mark fiddled with his flat cap and folded his arms. Kirsty didn't stop patrolling the perimeter for a second, too consumed with whatever was on her tablet.

"Well, that clears that up," Kirsty said, directing her eyes at Em. "Do you have an answer for me? I think my terms are fair. I've spent the last few days painstakingly rearranging the market's relaunch for *this* Friday, which gives us the crucial final weekend before Christmas sales. Now that we're able to promote things *properly*, the profit from the market will help us all keep paying rent here. Even at the reduced rate that I proposed, if we take in more members, it'll only mean more income for you in the long run."

"I'll have to think about it."

"What does that mean?"

"It means she'll think about it," Claire said, a little louder than she'd intended.

Kirsty stared down at her, and Claire felt like she was being assessed by a robot that had identified a bug in the system. If Kirsty knew Em at all, she'd know money was the last thing on the planet that she cared about. Out of the corner of her eye, Claire caught Mark smirking. Scott and Carol seemed to have checked out – if they'd ever really checked in.

Before the conversation could loop back around in

another series of dead ends, they were interrupted by a door slamming upstairs. Moments later, Bianca, the woman from the market with the icy blonde hair, marched in. She was walking so fast, the layers of her white chiffon dress floated around her like an ethereal snow queen's gown. It had slipped Claire's mind to confirm if Larry Evans' daughter Bianca was the same Bianca from Bianca's Boutique.

"Ah, Bianca, so nice of you to join us," Kirsty said. "You didn't reply to my email about whether you intend to stay here on a long-term basis."

"You, shut up," Bianca demanded, jabbing her finger in Kirsty's direction. She turned the pointed figure to Mark. "And you, where are they?"

To Claire's surprise, Kirsty stopped pacing. She seemed to be focusing all her energy on preventing her lips from wobbling into tears. She whipped around, leaving Claire to stare at Mark's confused yet amused smile. He looked just as he had done that morning with the trolley – but had his teddy bear smile always seemed so smug?

"You'll have to be more specific," Mark said. "And they? I'm assuming you're not talking about my mother's will in the plural. Which reminds me … while I'm here, does anyone know where the will is?"

The question came out less pointed than at the chippy, and that he asked it so publicly surprised Claire.

"Forget the will!" Bianca cried, tossing her arms out. "Where are my father's paintings? They're not in the attic, so somebody must have moved them. Which one of you was it?"

Claire almost wished her luck in getting an answer from this bunch.

"Maybe Anne moved them?" Carol suggested after a long silence.

"They were there the morning of the craft fair," Bianca said, her rage unwavering. "I demanded that Anne tell me where the paintings were being kept, and I've been checking on them to ensure their safety. I suspected their numbers were thinning. On the morning of the craft fair, I discovered evidence that Anne planned to sell the paintings to cash in on my father's legacy even more than she already had."

A collective sigh rippled around the room, hinting that this accusation had been flung about numerous times.

"The paintings are *not* in the attic," Bianca stated again. "Isn't *anyone* going to say anything?"

"It's not important right now," Kirsty said, giving a dismissive wave of her hand. However, she wasn't looking in Bianca's direction at all. "Em, can you at least confirm if we have permission to hold the market here?"

"Oh, I—"

"Forget the market." Bianca took a few more steps so

that she was in the middle of the scattered circle dotted around the room. "My father – Larry Evans – is more important than your craft fair. These paintings are his legacy, and at this moment in time, I don't know where most of them are. If we don't find them, this won't end well for any of you."

"*Most* of the paintings?" Scott said. "You said they'd *all* gone."

"There were a few left," Bianca said with a nod, "but the numbers have been dwindling ever since we got here, and there's at least three-quarters less than there were on the morning of the market."

"So, there's a quarter left?" Carol chipped in, half under her breath. "First, there's *none*, then a *few*, then a *quarter*. Which is it?"

"Aren't any of you hearing me?" Bianca hissed, looking around the room. "The paintings are gone, and the thief has to have been one of you."

"One of us," Carol corrected. "We're a collective."

"*The* Collective," Kirsty corrected in turn. "I don't have a clue about your father's paintings. For all I know, you've taken them and are accusing us to shift the blame. You're good at that."

"Yeah," Carol said before Bianca could fire back. "You're giving quite the performance now. Bravo. And the Oscar goes to. You've only ever been here to take those paintings. It's all you've cared about since the moment you arrived. I knew it, and Anne knew it. And I know Scott feels the same."

Carol looked around the room for support, but none came. Even Scott had a look of 'don't drag me into this' written across his sullen features.

"Is that so?" Bianca asked, her voice taking on a sudden eerie calmness. "You knew your best friend so well, did you?"

"Like the back of my hand."

"That same best friend whom you asked for a loan of money to help clear the debts your dear departed husband left you?"

"How dare you!"

"The same *best friend* who refused you and hung you out to dry while she lived a life of luxury off my father's fortune?"

The revelation that Carol had asked Anne for money – and that Anne had denied her – silenced the room, and Claire could barely believe what she was witnessing. For a group that called themselves The Collective, she'd never seen anything less collected. The Disjointed might have been more apt.

"You're only upset because your dad left everything to Anne instead of you," Scott said, standing up. "I'm tired of all this shouting. I have work to do. Some of us can't rely on the possibility of a market to keep the bills paid."

Scott excused himself, and Bianca wasted no time in

following him. Carol scurried out too, but Kirsty and Mark didn't look like they planned on moving, so Claire and Em wandered into the entrance hallway as doors closed on the landing above.

"This house does things to people," Em whispered. "You saw it drive Diane to murder my grandmother, and I watched it destroy Opal's life. It's too big. Too perfect. When people stay here, they don't want to leave, but it's the one thing they should do. Look at what it's doing to them all. How many more people must die here?"

"For what it's worth, I don't think it's just this house," Claire said. "They all followed Anne here. There's a pretty good chance she brought her murderer with her. Maybe it was only a matter of time. If not here, it would have happened somewhere else."

"Scott is from around here," Em reminded her. "I realised just now, being in his company, that I'd seen him several times over the summer, back when he had some facial hair, walking up and down the path near the canal. He slept on the benches a few nights. I offered to let him spend a night or two on my boat so he could get cleaned up, but he didn't take me up on it, and he moved on. I only recognised him today because of his height. The taller of us tend to be more memorable."

"Considering where he is now, you could call it a rags to riches story." Claire scanned the doors on the landing. Scott wasn't the only one needing money, as Bianca had just exposed. "If these paintings really are missing, there's a chance Anne died to clear a path to get them out. If they've even left the house, that is. There must be enough hiding places in a building this big."

"I spent enough of my life avoiding this place, so as not to know the nooks and crannies all too well, but your friend, Sally, has a copy of the blueprints with the house documents. We could go and have a look?"

"I'd like to see the attic where the paintings were being kept. If they were moved, they had to be moved somehow. A house this big, full of this many people, in the middle of a park? I can't imagine it was an easy task."

"That door there." Em pointed. "I'll go to the estate agents for a copy of the plans. The fresh air will do me good. I can only spend so long in a place with such dark energy."

"I don't blame you," Claire said, a shiver running over her shoulders as she looked around. "I feel it too."

———

THE NARROW STAIRCASE UP TO THE ATTIC ALSO HAD DARK energy because the bulb didn't work. With only a distant, faint light to guide her, Claire pulled herself up the steep steps with the help of the handrail. Enough dust to give her mother a heart attack covered the steps, though a path of footprints cast in the grubby layers suggested somewhat regular use. The lightbulb was high enough that it would have taken a ladder to unscrew and change it, and from the burnt-out glass of the bulb, it had blown around the time the stairs were last swept.

Claire hauled herself onto the top step and into the attic. Unlike the small space above her flat, the attic above Starfall House could have been an entire family home. The bright morning light streamed through the gaps in the tiles, illuminating the swirling particles in the air. On the far side, a round window she'd never noticed from the ground looked out at the park. The snowy vista drew her in, especially as the observatory on the top of the hill was perfectly positioned in the window.

"Hello?" a voice called out from the shadows.

Claire half jumped out of her skin – the reasonable response to a voice coming from the depths of a dusty attic. Looking away from the near-blinding brightness of the window, Claire squinted into the dark. Bianca's white dress glowed, almost a light source unto itself. She was perched on a wooden crate, her knees drawn tight into herself.

"Sorry, I didn't mean to scare you," Bianca said, all her earlier anger depleted.

"It's what I get for being nosey." Claire abandoned the window and approached Bianca. There were similar crates like the one she was sitting on stacked behind her. "Are these the remaining paintings?"

Bianca slid off the box and nodded. "This whole corner was filled with them when we first moved in. I kept telling Anne they were vanishing, but she said it was impossible, and that I was only trying to make her life difficult."

"You said you found something that suggested she wanted to sell the paintings?"

"Yes, on the morning of the craft fair. After I came to check on the paintings and knew I wasn't imagining them going missing, I confronted Anne. She tried to brush me off, so I went into her room to find something I could use as proof."

Bianca tugged a canvas from the crate and held it out. Like the pictures Claire had seen, hollow-eyed faces screamed out from rust-coloured geometric shapes. In person, the mountainous texture of the acrylic paints gave the painting more life. However, it didn't stop Claire from feeling unsettled, which she knew was the intention.

"What did you find?" Claire asked.

"Emails on her laptop," Bianca said. "Reaching out to buyers, responding to buyers. She was selling off his paintings, and I could do nothing about it. Scott was right. My father left everything to her. My father always had the view that inheritance spoiled children. He wanted me to make my own way. Pushed me to do it. I gave painting a try, but I could never match him." She ran a hand through her hair. "My father was a distant man. Overly critical, not just of himself but everyone. He was never satisfied. He never seemed happy a day in his life, yet I daresay that's what made him such a good artist. Anne didn't understand his work well enough to respect what needed to be done to preserve his legacy. After my father died and everything was signed over to her, she cashed in on selling his house and everything in it before the ink was dry."

"Your father must have trusted her enough to leave her everything."

"My father was an old *fool*, and I don't mind saying it." Bianca let the painting slide back into the box. "Whenever I challenged him on anything, he knocked me back, shut me down. When Anne challenged his entire art career in a gallery one random afternoon, he married her. He wasn't in his right mind. My mother had only recently died, and I think he knew he wouldn't have long left, what with the way he lived. Late nights, early mornings, often at the same time. In the days after my mother died, he'd paint in his studio until his hands were so curled he could barely pry the paintbrush from them. Anne barely saw him. She ran around town, living off the prestige of being married to a famous artist, professing to be this great art lover, when she'd never even heard of my father until that day in the gallery. For him, she was someone to bring the cups of tea and keep the house ticking over."

Bianca gave a sour smile and turned away. "Pushed me out into the big world, and I had to make something of myself on my own. I started my own clothing line from nothing. I had boutiques up and down the country, and I never got so much as a 'well done' from him. Seeing how he was with Kirsty made it even more baffling."

"Your father knew Kirsty?"

"She was his *protégé*," she said, rolling her eyes. "He met her at a college art show at which he'd been asked to show his face. Fell in love with her work and swore she was the next great thing in art. Took her under his wing, but her career never went anywhere. Very few artists make a living from their work. I should never have taken pity on her and given her a job."

"Kirsty used to work for you?"

"Kirsty was my assistant before she was Anne's. I fired her for being a controlling know-it-all. Failed art career or not, having Larry Evans tell Kirsty she was the next great thing had her believing it. I did her a favour by giving her a job, but she had ideas above her station. I wouldn't be surprised if she took the paintings to get back at me for firing her. Anne was going to follow suit soon. I could tell Kirsty's ways were getting to her like they got to me."

"She would have had easy access to Anne's laptop," Claire pointed out. "She could have been sending those emails on Anne's behalf."

"I didn't think of that." Bianca turned to the window and stared out. The snow had started while they'd been talking, and the fluffy flakes now blocked the view of the observatory. "Wherever they are, I hope they're safe. It took his death for me to realise his art was the only way I'd ever understood him. They're my connection to my father, and the value of his work proves I'm not the only one who finds it vital. He sold very few of his paintings throughout his lifetime. They deserve to be in museums, where people can see them. That's all I wanted for them. I tried to make Anne see that, but she overreacts – overreacted – to everything."

"I had noticed," Claire said, remembering Anne's outrageous overreaction that had led to her involvement in this mess. "She seemed upset before I got to her."

"I noticed that when I talked to her too," Bianca said, as though recalling the fact just now. "It was around the time people started arriving. She'd just come out of Mark's room, and she was all flustered like she was holding back tears."

"Mark's technically your step-brother?"

"We never blended like a family in that way. I never looked at Anne as a mother. I didn't respect her. She was a fake. A phoney. She went from dressing like an estate agent in her sixties to Yoko Ono overnight, and I know my father thought her a fool because of it. She will have noticed how sickly he was in his final years. It was hard not to. I thought she was marrying him to secure her future after being widowed. I told my father as much on his wedding day, but he either didn't want to listen or didn't care. She may have got what she wanted then, but now she's dead because of it, my father's paintings are missing, and his dream of The Collective is an embarrassment to his memory as an artist."

"The Collective was your father's idea?"

"His vision of a life centred around art. The way he talked about it made it sound like a hippie commune, but he was sure it was the way to live. The way to make art. Ironic, because I could hardly make a peep growing up so he could stay 'in the zone', but my father was nothing if not a contradiction." Bianca turned from the window and looked at the remaining paintings. "My feelings for him are a contradiction, even now. I have few truly heart-warming memories of my father, yet I know his art deserves better than to go missing from a dusty attic and for no one to care about it."

"Have you spoken to the police about it?"

"I did mention my suspicions during my interview, but now that so few remain, maybe it's the time for them to do something. Thank you for listening to me, Claire. You're the first person who's taken me seriously about this. I couldn't believe Anne was spreading all those rumours about you at the fair. If my father was a contradiction, she was a straight-up hypocrite, accusing you of selling factory-bought candles."

"Anne's were factory bought?"

Bianca nodded. "Saw boxes upon boxes of them in her bedroom, and judging by the label, they were made in China. I could tell your candles were handmade, as were the items on my stall. I wouldn't be surprised if Anne didn't craft a single one of the items she was selling. The woman was fake to the core. All she wanted was attention, and this was her way to get it. Karma had its way with her, in the end."

Bianca set off to the staircase, creating her own wind with the chiffon layers of her dress as she floated through the dusty streams of light. A somewhat dramatic exit after an even more dramatic closing line, certainly, but Claire had one more question.

"Anne would cut off her nose to spite her face," Claire called after Bianca, running through the cloud of dust whipped up by the movement of the dress with none of Bianca's grace. "That's what you said that morning when I thought Anne had stuck me in the corner on purpose. What did you mean by it?"

Bianca hesitated at the top of the stairs and glanced over her shoulder. "I offered to work with Anne. I would manage the paintings, get them out to galleries to be seen, and we could split the money. It was an excellent idea that would have been best for both of us, but she chose to cling to them. She couldn't get past the fact he'd left them to *her* like they were some precious treasures she'd *earned*. Like I said – karma."

Claire followed Bianca down the narrow staircase and out into the landing. The fashion designer continued down the stairs, but Claire lingered and watched her descend, looking less ethereal and more like a ghost the further away she walked.

"Claire," Carol hissed from her bedroom door in her red cardigan. It was open a crack, and her clay-covered hands were held up awkwardly. "Don't believe anything she said."

"You heard us?"

"Almost every word. There must be a duct running along somewhere. I can't believe she had the nerve to call Anne fake. Has she *seen* herself? You know she used to be an actress."

"I thought she was a designer?"

"She was an actress before she was a designer," Carol said, looking somewhat pleased with herself. "Or should I say a failed actress before she was a failed designer? She forgot to mention that her company went bankrupt. If Kirsty is to be believed, she was the glue holding Bianca's company together. For Bianca to call anyone a failed anything is the pot calling the kettle black. And for her to mention *my* money troubles." Carol pulled her red cardigan in as she glanced up and down the empty hallway, not seeming to notice the clay she was spreading on the fabric. "It's true. I asked Anne for a loan. Just a loan. I would have paid her back. But she was just coming to grips with having so much money. I didn't hold it against her. It *never* affected our friendship. But if Bianca had been in good standing with Anne, she'd have asked for money too. She was living off her father's handouts. All that about not being supported? Anne told me *everything*. Bianca would mention her mother to upset her father, and then tell him about her business woes. Those loans were never paid back, and now she wants to get her hands on his paintings. Her father didn't disinherit her because he wanted her to make her own way. He didn't leave her a thing because he didn't trust her with it. He trusted Anne. She'd never have sold those paintings."

Carol ducked back into her bedroom, closing the door behind herself, having thrown into doubt everything Bianca had just told Claire in the attic. She'd sensed embellishment in places, but now she didn't know if any of it could be trusted. Not that she knew if Carol could be trusted either. Or any of them. Claire looked at the double doors belonging to Mark's room, but like Em, she felt the need to get out of Starfall House.

"Got a copy of the plans," Em called as they crossed paths by the fountain. "I'll have a look at them. Learn anything useful?"

"I spoke to Bianca and Carol. The more I learn, the less clear the picture looks."

"Well, I'm happy to clear up one picture," Em said, patting Claire's cheek on her way past. "I just saw Ryan, and he told me to tell you to check your phone."

Leaving the park, Claire smiled at the text from Ryan.

'Dinner at my place tonight? (Please say yes.)'

Claire wasted no time replying with 'Absolutely yes.' When she hit send, some of the heaviness she'd been feeling in her chest floated away. With plans for later and a closed shop, there was only one place to spend her Sunday afternoon.

CHAPTER EIGHT

*C*laire trudged through the thick snow, glad of her ankle-high walking boots. No cars had attempted the lane yet, leaving her to disturb the soft layer with each satisfying step. At this time of year, the snow and the fully decorated cul-de-sac at the end of the lane always made her feel like a kid again.

"We get snow but once or twice a year, dear," Claire heard her father say as she let herself in through the front door. "Sometimes we don't get it at all. It'll be gone by morning."

Claire announced herself on the doorstep with a stomp of her boots. A mountain of Christmas decorations lay at the foot of the stairs. Starfall House's attic contained paintings, but Claire's parents' attic had decoration sets of every colour associated with the festive season. They'd pulled out silver and lilac this year, though, from the number of tags, her mother had bought many new items. She always did.

"They're saying it'll last until Christmas," Janet said, untangling a length of silver tinsel in the kitchen. "Oh, hello, Claire. Get yourself warm in here. I was just telling your father that if this snow doesn't melt soon, the offices I clean will close, everyone will work from home, and I won't need to clean the offices. I've already lost the craft fair job that was supposed to keep me busy. I can't lose my bread-and-butter customers. How can I expand Janet's Angels across Lancashire if I go bust in my first year?"

"I'm sure it won't come to that," Alan said, accepting a kiss on the cheek from Claire as he worked on the crossword in the newspaper. "It's a little snow, and you already have bookings on the calendar up until spring, my love. No need to worry. Have you shown Claire your new logo yet?"

Janet flapped a finger in the direction of the sideboard. "I finally got around to having something official made. Found a local company. Northash Design Agency. Took a while, but what do you think?"

Claire scooped up a sheet of paper showing a logo in different situations: on a t-shirt, the side of a van, a business card. They couldn't be real – her mother's van was white and not blue – but Claire was impressed by how professional the mock-ups looked.

The logo, on the other hand, left a little to be desired. A cartoonish yellow halo hovered above 'Janet's Angels', with wings sprouting from either side. The hand-drawn style was reminiscent of a tattoo.

"Your father stared at the thing too," Janet said, rattling the tinsel as the unravelling sped up. "Say something. I paid good money for it."

"It sort of looks like it's for a jolly funeral home."

"That's what *I* said!"

"That's what your father said."

"If it's not too late for changes, you might want to have them add that it's a cleaning company."

"I'll call them, but given how long it took to get that, I could be waiting months." Janet crossed into the dining room area and tucked the tinsel behind a watercolour painting of the house, a gift from Ryan for Janet's last birthday. "I just want everything to be perfect. To what do we owe the honour today, anyway, Claire? Stumbled upon another dead body?"

"Not yet," Claire said, finally feeling warm enough to unwind her scarf. "But I did stumble across a couple of suspects. Oh, and Ryan's wife, Maya, who just happens to be right here in Northash at this very moment."

"We know," Janet said, giving her a stern look followed by a sigh. "And I can't believe you didn't call to tell us. I wanted to call immediately, but your father *insisted* we give you some space."

"What your mother *means* to say is we wanted to be there for you while also respecting that you're a grown-up."

"I'm fine," Claire said, to which they both raised their brows. "Honestly. How did you know?"

"Your Granny Greta was out walking Spud, and she saw a woman leaving Ryan's place last night," Alan said. "She jumped to the wrong conclusions until Ryan set her straight."

"She also said she was beautiful. Her exact words were 'Eva Longoria in athletic wear.'"

"Spot on, I'd say." Claire shifted in her chair, trying not to let the shrinking feeling take over. "It was only a matter of time before she made contact somehow, especially after she sent Amelia that birthday card. Christmas seems as good a time as any."

"Do you think she'll still be here by then?" Janet asked, not hiding her frown. "Surely, she can sign the divorce papers, hop on a plane, and run back to that friend of Ryan's she left him for. What was his name?"

"Will. And I don't know if they're still together. I don't know much, other than that she's here and she already hates me."

"She said that, little one?"

"She didn't need to." Claire pointed two fingers at her

eyeballs. "And it's also not as simple as that, Mum. They have kids together who need answers. Ryan needs answers. I don't think this is a flying visit. Anyway, I didn't come here to talk about my relationship woes."

"I'm honestly just glad you have a relationship to have woes about, dear," Janet said, filling the kettle to the brim. "If you two are about to disappear off to the shed, I'm making you some hot water bottles and broth. I won't have you catching your death in the name of your investigations."

WITH A SCALDING HOT WATER BOTTLE SUITABLY CRAMMED between her t-shirt and jumper, Claire settled into her plant pot in the corner of the shed and in full view of the heater. She let her mother's vegetable broth, a similar colour to Ryan's paint water, fall off her spoon and back into the steaming bowl. Her father settled into his tatty office chair at his potting table and took a brave slurp.

"Salty?"

"Always is." Alan clapped his tongue against the roof of his mouth. "She's on salt watch with everything else, but it's fair game when it comes to stock cubes."

"You're going to have to tell her one of these years that you don't like her winter broth. She only makes it because she thinks you love it."

"I said I liked it once sometime in the 1980s," he said with a chuckle. "I don't have the heart to admit I've been lying ever since. Every winter, it's all about the broth and vitamin C. I'm likely to start emitting an orange glow, given how many supplements she has me on."

"Start? You're practically radioactive, Dad."

"I don't doubt it, little one." He took a bigger mouthful. "But that's how your mother shows love. Are you sure you don't want to talk about what's happening with Ryan?"

Claire lifted the spoon closer to her mouth, but again it went back into the bowl. She considered pouring her heart out to her father, admitting her worries and fears, but like with Damon and Sally, it didn't come. She wasn't sure she was ready to say them out loud, so instead, she told him about her visit to Starfall House.

"So, what do you think?" she asked after rounding off the story with Carol and her clay-covered hands. "Any of them sound guilty to you?"

"Details about each suggest any of them could be behind this. The police are no closer to pinning down any concrete evidence left at the crime scene, although they have narrowed down the type of footwear used to crush your candle." He paused to slurp more broth before abandoning the bowl on the desk. "It seems to have been the heel of a boot."

"Men's or women's?" she asked. "Size?"

"They haven't been able to specify, given that it's only a partial print, but it seems to be a standard walking boot." Alan drummed his fingers on the chair arm, nodding down at her walking boots. "Another angle to frame you?"

Claire shook her head. "I was wearing trainers that morning. Must be a coincidence."

"Ramsbottom said he was gathering samples of shoes at the house, so maybe that'll pin it down. Until then, I want to know what *you* think. You told me what happened but not what you think about it. You saw their body language and how they acted with each other. What did you pick up on?"

"That there seemed to be no harmony between any of them," she said, thinking about the argument in the library. "Kirsty and Bianca had friction immediately, which Bianca only confirmed. When I spoke to Kirsty, she made out she had a great working relationship with Anne while also complaining about how Anne ran things. Kirsty also seems to be the one who wants to carry on business as usual, although I get that feeling from all of them."

"Is the assistant your prime suspect?"

Claire immediately saw Mark's face in her mind. His plump-cheeked smile, jolly on first meeting and then smug, had taken on a sinister twist in her mind, like something resembling a Larry Evans painting.

"No," she said. "The son. I need to talk to Mark again. I think there's more to him than meets the eye. Both Kirsty and Carol insist that Mark was always hounding his mother about money, and he openly admitted to wanting to find her will. With Anne out of the way, it would all be his."

"*If* Anne left her inherited fortune to him," he said, his hands coming together at the fingertips. "Larry Evans didn't leave *his* fortune to his daughter, so who's to say Anne left hers to her son? You said Bianca saw Anne leaving Mark's room on the morning of the fair close to tears, and you saw evidence of that yourself later on."

"He did seem rather critical of her in the brief interaction I saw between them," Claire said with an agreeing nod. "So, there could be a will, and it's all to go to someone else? One of them could be hiding it."

"Including Mark."

"You're right. If Carol thinks Bianca is double bluffing about not knowing where the paintings are, what's to say he's not doing the same?"

Claire pulled out her phone and searched 'Bianca Evans' online. She scrolled past a few of the results. One was for her boutique. She clicked the link, but the website led to an error page. Back on the results, she came across an IMDb page.

"Carol was right about her being an actress," Claire confirmed. "Starred as Hippie Protestor Two in a 1993 episode of *The Bill*, Unnamed Corpse in a 2002 *Midsomer Murders*, and as a character called Professor Scales in a 2004 straight-to-DVD film called *Siege of the Seven Foot Snakes*, which has an impressive one and a half stars across six reviews."

"Quite the varied career."

"Explains her dramatics," Claire said, tapping her phone in her palm as she stared at the shed wall. "The question is, is she dramatic because she was an actress, or was she an actress because she's dramatic?"

"Excellent question, little one. What about the others? The friend? The boyfriend?"

"Both seem to have needed money. Em thinks she saw Scott sleeping on a bench this past summer, and Carol admitted to asking for a loan." Claire thought back to her first conversation with Carol. "It could be about more than money. I think I picked up on some jealousy from Carol toward Anne about her having a boyfriend. She said something along the lines of Anne not appreciating what she had in Scott."

"Hmm." He pressed his fingertips together again and nodded slowly. "You've got plenty to think about, little one. If this were my investigation, the first point of my plan would be speaking to each of them again to try and further explain the thoughts behind how you're connecting the dots. Though be warned, given the accusations, they might not be as forthcoming with information the second time around."

"Noted. And the rest of the points of your how-many-part plan?"

Alan considered his response. "Three. First, I'd speak with each suspect again. Second, I'd want to find the shoe that caused the boot print. The killer has been good at covering their tracks, so the original shoe could be long gone, but I'd still hunt down a copy of it. It might help trigger someone's memory." Alan reached out and took the bowl from Claire before ditching the contents of their broth leftovers in a stray pot of compost. "And third, I'd want to know where those paintings have gone. If Bianca is right and Ramsbottom isn't taking their disappearance seriously, then I don't mind calling him a fool. The combined worth of those paintings could buy Starfall House twice over. If Anne meant to sell them and there are emails proving it, it could lead to the paintings being found, and perhaps the person behind selling them. And if that person wasn't working on Anne's behalf, it's certainly someone who wanted to appear as though Anne was the seller."

"Why would someone go to the trouble?"

"Anne's name popped up several times in my initial research on Larry Evans. It's no secret in the art world that she inherited the paintings. A few people said it was a license to print money, but Anne was quoted several times stating she wouldn't sell the paintings."

"Anne's precious treasures, according to Bianca. So, somebody could have been using Anne's email account without her knowing to legitimise the sale?"

"Bingo." Alan pushed himself out of the chair and grabbed his cane. "Now, let's get back into the house. You can revisit Starfall House later, but first, I beg you to stay for at least another couple of hours. I need your support. We're putting up the tree, and you know how your mother gets with the baubles."

LATER THAT AFTERNOON, ALONE WITH THE CATS IN HER flat, Claire stepped back and assessed the finished Christmas tree in the corner by the window. She'd picked this one – of the three to choose from in her mother's attic – for the preinstalled lights, though she'd almost been tempted by one with artificial snow on the tips. The lights twinkled in the branches of the classic green fir bristles, making her glad she'd gone for the red-and-white scheme. It matched the shop's candy cane display downstairs, which had taken so much effort that she'd avoided decorating the flat all month. She'd left her parents' house looking like Santa's grotto, suitably inspired to finally decorate her own flat for her first

Christmas there. Unlike her mother, she'd managed it all without pulling out a ruler to check that the baubles were all 'correctly spaced for maximum visual impact'.

"I better not catch either of you climbing this thing," Claire ordered Domino and Sid, curled around each other on the sofa. She dug a hand into their soft, warm bellies, and they rolled onto their backs in unison. "With how the weather's turned, I'll turn you into a nice pair of slippers if I catch you up there."

Claire considered staying on her sofa for the rest of the evening, waiting for her dinner date at Ryan's while rubbing the cat's bellies and staring at the changing lights of the tree, but it didn't take long for her father's three-point plan to start circling.

Interview suspects.

Find shoe.

Find paintings.

The shoe would be tricky. The police knew it was a walking boot, so it must have left a print that could be matched to something online. Still, without a picture from Ramsbottom, she'd be browsing with no idea what she was looking for.

The paintings would be the trickiest. Her first instinct was to gain access to Anne's laptop. With them all living under the same roof, any of The Collective could have accessed Anne's laptop as easily as Bianca. Claire was confident the laptop would be in police custody.

Around half past three, as the pale blue sky began to fade to a creamy yellow, Claire pushed herself off the sofa and into her boots. There was one thing she could do. Leaving the cats with the Christmas tree, she set off to Starfall Park for the second time that day.

"I mean it," Claire reminded them. "Slippers!"

———

CLAIRE HURRIED THROUGH THE VICTORIAN conservatory at the back of Starfall House and into the kitchen. She waited for the heat to wrap around her, but it didn't come. It was almost as freezing inside as out. She walked through a cloud of her condensing breath and into the entrance hall. There wasn't a light on in the place, the only illumination the hazy glow of the setting twilight sun. Instinct drove her toward a flickering light in the library. She let out a sigh of relief when she heard crackling flames.

Scott was in a high-backed chair by the fire, his feet propped on a footstool – wearing slippers made of sheep's wool and not cat fur. A laptop lit up his face, and he didn't notice her until Claire was almost at the chair opposite him. His extreme concentration faded instantly, and he looked at her with strained eyes. A shadow of purple circled red rings drawn around bloodshot pupils.

He looked like Damon after a lengthy *Dawn Ship* tournament.

"Bit nippy in here," Claire said, pointing to the chair by the fire. "Mind if I join you?"

"Not at all." Scott's feet darted off the footstool, and he sat up straight. He placed the laptop on a side table. "Kirsty's taken control of the thermostat in the name of cost-cutting. She says she wants us all to stay here, but it feels like she's trying to freeze us out. Couldn't stand to be in my room for another second. Found a stack of logs in the cellar." He threw another couple onto the flames, and the comforting air warmed the bite from Claire's cheeks. "They're saying the snow's here to stay. Northash's very own mini ice age."

"I swear I hear that yearly, but the snow always melts eventually." Claire tugged off her gloves between her teeth and settled into the chair, sensing her opportunity to dig deeper with Scott. "You're from around these parts, aren't you? Not Northash, but close. Your accent is Lancashire, but I can't quite place it."

"I'm from near Blackpool way," he said, tossing a gesture in the direction of the observatory as though Blackpool wasn't at least an hour's drive away. "I've moved further east as I've grown older. One of the joys of being freelance is moving around as much as I please."

Claire realised she didn't know what Scott did; so far,

his role in The Collective hadn't stretched beyond being Anne's boyfriend.

"Freelance?"

"Graphic designer," he said, lifting the lid of his laptop a little. "Well, an all-round digital artist. Got in on the ground with web designing back in the nineties, and I've never done anything else. With everything going on, I'd rather do anything but write code for a website, but I had deadlines before Anne died, and they haven't vanished."

Claire squinted at the bright screen, recognising the chippy menu, although it looked slightly different from the current design. She'd left him in the chippy yesterday afternoon, rubbing the corner of the menu. He worked quick.

"You're designing for the chippy next to my shop?" Claire asked.

"I am. And since you brought it up, I had a little look at your candle website." He edged forward, scratching the side of his face as he drew a breath through his teeth. "Did you make it yourself?"

"Damon helped," she said, "but mostly. Why?"

"Listen." He drew closer to the fire, and Claire couldn't help but lean in. "It's a good start. Really, it is, but I think it has some issues."

Claire gulped. She was proud of the website they'd put together. It hadn't been easy to get it to where it was.

"Issues?" she asked. "It's quite new."

"Then it's the best time to fix things. They're small issues. Accessibility, placement, SEO. Tweaks that can make a big difference." He reached inside the dressing gown that barely went past the thighs of his long legs, and pulled a wallet from another layer. "I really think I could help take things to the next level. How many orders are you getting a week?"

"We had thirty-two last week."

"I could double it." He held out the card between his fingers. "Triple, even. I'll even give you a discount, from one local business owner to another."

Claire accepted the card and turned it over in her hand. Northash Design Agency. "You designed my mum's logo?"

"I did?" His brows went up.

"Janet's Angels?"

"Janet's Angels. Janet's Angels." He clicked his fingers as though he couldn't recall. "Ah, the cleaning company. Yes, I did. Great woman. Sweet."

Claire wondered if there was another Janet with an angel-themed cleaning company out there. She tucked the card away without mentioning that she hadn't thought much of the logo.

"I also did some work for The Plough," he offered. "Designed their Merry Crispmas packet."

"Really?"

"Yep." He gave a proud smile before offering his open

134

palms. "You don't have to decide now, but you've got my card. I really think I could bring a lot of value to what you've already built."

Scott had the charm of any good salesman – she'd never seen him so animated – but a whiff of desperation clawed at the edges.

"I'll think about it," she said, but she hadn't come to talk about upgrading her website. "You know my friend Em?"

"The owner of this house?" He tilted his head from side to side. "I wouldn't say I know her, but yes, I know of her. Why?"

"You know she lives on that narrowboat?"

"Down by the canal." He nodded. "Yes, why?"

"She said she saw you sleeping on a bench over the summer." Scott's expression froze. "I'm not judging," Claire added, her turn to hold up her palms. "I was just wondering if that's when you first came to Northash. I'm still trying to figure out all the pieces of Anne's life, and, well, I've heard that some people think you're playing a game."

"Mark, you mean," he said flatly. "And yes, I slept on the bench once."

"Em said she saw you a few times."

"Okay, so it was a couple of times." He laughed, though his cheeks had turned red. "Like I said, I move around a lot. Mark thinks my being here is a huge conspiracy to steal his mother's fortune, but that's not the case. My previous business went bust, and I was ready for a new start somewhere else. Northash seemed as nice a place as any. It was only until I got my first job here. Designed some flyers for Lilac Gifts. As soon as I earned some money, I lodged with a nice woman down by the mechanics."

"Greta?"

"Yes." He squinted at the quick recall. "Have you lodged there too?"

"That's my gran. She's rented out her spare room for as long as I can remember. Pays for her sunny holidays."

"This village really is small. First your mother, now your gran. And she was hardly home. I was something of a live-in dog sitter, truth be told, but I was only there for a month before I came here."

"That quick?"

"Anne and I fell in love," he said, staring into the fire. "We met in The Park Inn. It was your gran who suggested it. She said that if I was to go on a first date, I shouldn't go to The Plough because it would be full of nosey people."

"That sounds like my gran, and she's right."

"There was hardly anybody in The Park Inn, including the woman I was there to meet, Sinead. We met on an app, but she stood me up and blocked me. Dating was a lot easier back when I was younger, which is why

Anne and I hit it off. That classic tale of bumping into each other in a pub. I was at the bar, alone. She came in, sat next to me, and the rest is history."

"Sounds like you hit it off quickly."

"Anne was in Northash for a house viewing. Asked if I knew much about the park and the area. I told her I didn't know much, but I shared what I'd found out about where everything was. I said the people were friendly. We still managed to talk late into the night. I can't even remember what about. We just had that spark. Despite what Mark thinks, I didn't know she meant this was the house she was viewing. We were already in love when she admitted she'd inherited a fortune. It didn't change anything." He frowned into the fire. "I can't get my head around it being over, just like that. We had a good thing going on for a moment."

Every muscle in Scott's body seemed to relax, and despite his height, he looked frail slumped in the chair. He glanced at the laptop, but the last thing he needed was to continue working.

"I'm sorry," he said, picking up the laptop and standing. "I think I need to go back up to my room. It's been quite a tough few days."

"Of course," Claire said, joining him in standing. "Don't suppose you know if the police took Anne's laptop?"

"Her laptop?" Scott searched his mind for a moment

but shook his head. "I'm not sure. I haven't been in her room since everything happened. It might still be in there. Is it important?"

"Bianca thought Anne was trying to sell the paintings. Do you know anything about that?"

"I meant it when I said Anne didn't talk to me about that. She never wanted to talk about her will, the money, the inheritance, or the dead husband. We chose to live in the moment. Mark wouldn't know anything about that. He's stuck in the past. Look at him. He followed her all the way up here. He should have let her go, but he couldn't stand the thought of her being out of his sight. She can't stand being around him, even now."

Claire had assumed Scott was talking about Anne until the last few words and his use of the present tense. "Who can't stand being around him?"

"Kirsty."

"Why would Mark need to let Kirsty go?"

"Because they were engaged until a few months before everyone moved up here," he said, arching a brow as though Claire should have known. "Kirsty ended things, and he's taken it badly. Anne said he was a different man back then. Kinder, sweeter. All I've ever seen of him is his anger."

Scott left the library, and Claire lingered by the fire for a moment to consider her options. Of all the things she'd noticed, how had she missed such a connection between two suspects? She could turn the place upside down looking for a walking boot, or search Anne's bedroom for her laptop, but the police should have both of those covered if Ramsbottom was conducting the investigation properly.

Mark's room, however, was just at the top of the stairs, and from the red glow around the edge of the double doors leading to the biggest bedroom in the grand house, she'd caught him at home. Every suspect had pointed the finger at Mark somehow, and now it was time for him to answer for himself.

CHAPTER NINE

*C*laire took in the bedrooms as she padded across the soft carpet of the landing. Melancholic orchestral strings floated from Carol's door. Scott tapped on his keyboard next door. The room she'd seen Anne storm off to was next, with Kirsty on the end before Mark's room at the front of the house.

Kirsty's door was open, and she was talking loudly on the phone, stepping over the clothes strewn about as she paced from one side of the room to the other. Claire slowed as much as she could without making it evident that she was lingering.

"I know it's short notice," Kirsty said, cheerier than Claire had ever heard her, though her face was screwed up. "Plenty of people commented on how much they *loved* your soap stall. Yes, really. It would be a shame if you weren't here this coming weekend. No, you won't have to pay for your stall again, though there is a small commission fee to pay for overheads. I can assure you that if this is a success, there'll be a craft fair every season. Those who attend this coming weekend will have first refusal of stalls."

"Eavesdropping?"

Mark's voice caught Claire off-guard. He stood in the doorway of his room, the red glow lighting up his white dressing gown from behind. The robe was open enough to reveal that the hair wasn't limited to his face.

"I might be," Claire whispered, stepping away from Kirsty's room. "You're eavesdropping on me eavesdropping."

"I'm on my way to get a glass of water," Mark said, holding up an empty pint glass. "Please, don't let me stop you. Is she still begging all the stallholders to give her revival fair a chance?"

Claire nodded. The malice in Mark's voice was obvious now that she knew the connection. Kirsty's had been similar when she'd pointed the finger at Mark. He walked down the hall to the stairs, leaving his bedroom door wide open.

The curious red light flooding the room drew her in. A desk with a widescreen iMac and scattered photography equipment were the only hints that any time had passed since Claire's last visit to the room – to confront the housekeeper, Diane, about murdering Opal. On that occasion, she'd left the room with Diane's pocketknife held to her throat.

The red light was coming from a small bathroom. Dripping pictures hung on a washing line in front of the mirror. Claire gulped, not sure she wanted to know the subject of the shots, but nosiness got the best of her. She stepped into the bathroom and was relieved to see ten or so pictures of the park. There were artful shots of the snow-capped observatory, the compositions and lighting giving the structure an extra magnificence she'd never seen with her eyes. There was a shot of the robin on the marble fountain, a couple of the house, and one that made Claire reach up to pluck it down.

She laughed.

"Why did you close your eyes?" Mark's voice startled her again. She glanced in the mirror at him as he sipped from a full glass. "If there was ever a moment to be videoing something, it was then – though in this case, a picture really does say a thousand words."

Mark turned on a white bulb that cast out enough red light for her to see the picture clearly. With her gloved hands gripping the trolley, Claire careened toward the camera in a clenched-eyed blur. Her scarf trailed behind her, while her knees dipped in and ankles flared out at awkward angles on the ice.

"This might be frame-worthy," Claire said. "Not that

your other shots aren't impressive. Looks like there's a little more going on than pointing and clicking. Have you been into photography for long?"

"Ever since I left school. It used to be my passion."

"Used to be?"

"It became my job."

He offered a tight smile, taking the picture from Claire and clipping it back to the string. "I sold my company, and I've been trying to let the change of scenery reinspire me. It's part of the reason I came up here."

Claire followed Mark out of the red bathroom. He reached around her and closed the door before going about the room, flicking on the many lamps. The room was so big that the light barely took a dent out of the dark now that the sun had set. The large window looking out over the park drew her in – or rather, the observatory did. The evening fog blurred the lights still on inside to soft cream orbs.

Claire recalled what Carol, Kirsty, and Scott had said about Mark. Carol had accused him of following because he didn't know how to let his mother go, and Scott accused him of following Kirsty. All three had mentioned his obsession with the will.

"Part of the reason?" Claire turned away from the window. Mark perched on his bed, leaning back on his elbows. "I got the impression you'd come up here to keep an eye on your mother."

"I had many reasons to want a fresh start," he said with a shrug. "But yes, that was also part of the reason. Someone needed to ensure she wasn't making bad decisions ... not that she ever listened to me about the sharks in the water."

"The sharks?"

"Don't you see them circling?" He pushed forward, leaning on his knees. "All of them. Carol, Scott, Bianca, Kirsty. They all wanted something from my mother."

"And you didn't?"

"All *I* wanted was for my mother to open her eyes and see how they all had *their* eyes on her fortune."

"Funnily enough, they've all said the same about you." Claire folded her arms, rocking back on her heels. "You've taken quite an interest in your mother's will."

"Wouldn't you do the same in my position?" Mark arched a brow. "Look, I don't want to speak out of turn, but it sounds like this isn't a social visit. Do you suspect me, Claire?"

Claire cleared her throat in response to the direct question. Mark's expression fell, the jolly teddy bear flipping into a sad one.

"Right," he said flatly before crossing the room. "So, they've all said *I'm* the one who wanted her money, yet I know I'm the only one who doesn't need it. Carol's husband left her broke, Bianca's fashion line bankrupted her, Scott limps from job to job, and Kirsty's been working for lodging and scraps since her painting career floundered."

Again, the venom was clear. Mark picked up his phone and, after a few taps, handed it to her. She took it and looked down at a mobile banking app showing a figure that dried her mouth.

£454,392.29.

"I started a corporate stock photography business when I was twenty-one," he explained. "I was one guy with a camera and a dream. When I sold the company nine years later, I had a team of twenty, a studio, and thousands of images selling daily. Are you okay?"

"Yep," Claire said hoarsely, handing the phone back. "I've just never seen so much money before."

"All from boring pictures of people in offices, grinning children brushing their teeth, women laughing while they eat salads. The sort of soulless filler that killed my passion for photography. Baffles me too, but it filled my bank account. Not sure if it's a fair exchange. I couldn't care less about getting my hands on my mother's money. I want to find her will because I'm convinced one of them twisted her ear to get their hands on everything – and maybe even killed her for it."

Mark tossed the phone onto the bedside table. It hit something metal, causing it to clatter onto the floorboards. Since she was closer to the fallen object, Claire bent to scoop it up – a single brass key attached to a shooting star keyring. Her gaze went to the window and the building looming on the hill above them.

"That's what I thought too," Mark said, joining her at the window. "I found it earlier, in the snow by the house. I've been waiting until dark to go give it a try. I'm dying to have a look around the place. The lights haven't been off since *that* day."

"Have the police searched it?"

"I haven't seen them up there." Mark looped his finger through the keyring and took it back from Claire. He gave it a tempting wiggle and, with a smile, said, "It's dark. Fancy some snooping?"

Mark's smile seemed as innocent as it had when they'd first met, but the Mark she'd overheard in the chippy crept back into her mind. She wasn't sure if the money in his account proved that he didn't murder his mother, but it did melt away some of the motives 'the sharks' had flung his way.

And she did want to see inside the observatory.

"Get dressed," Claire said, turning back to the window. "You'll catch your death going out there like that."

While Mark rummaged in the drawers behind her, Claire stared up the hill.

"Do you know the story behind the place?" Mark

called.

"It was built in the early twentieth century by Em's great-great-grandfather as a monument to a lost love," Claire explained, recalling the story Diane had told her. "He thought his deceased wife was among the stars, so he spent his days searching the skies for her."

"That's quite romantic."

"It drove him mad," Claire said, wrapping her arms around herself. "Hanged himself from one of the park's trees in the twenties."

"Oh."

Claire wasn't surprised Em didn't want anything to do with the house; she wasn't sure she did either. The last time she'd been standing in this spot, the window's glass had been missing thanks to Diane throwing a chair through it. The knife to the throat had followed. And then Diane had convinced Claire that she'd poisoned her before shoving her into the duck pond.

Maybe Starfall House was cursed.

At least she'd gone into the pond during the spring.

Claire looked at the pond. The ducks had moved on for the season, and she couldn't imagine how cold the water would be under the layer of ice reflecting the silvery moon.

"Ready?"

"Yeah," Claire replied, unable to look away from the duck pond. "What's that?"

"What's what?"

Claire squinted. The moon reflected off more than the ice, as it was still thin enough that the water was moving. Or rather, something could move *in* the water. Mark joined her at the window, holding a piece of photography equipment to his eye. He muttered something under his breath as he passed the item to Claire. Hands shaking, she tried to focus the telescope-like object on the glow in the middle of the pond. Claire was so engaged in this task that she didn't realise Mark had left her side until she saw him wading into the pond toward the ethereal swirl of white hair and fabric.

Mark rolled Bianca over. Her head lolled back, pallid face pointing directly at the lens. Claire let the lens fall from her eye as she ran across the room – though she didn't know why she was rushing.

Bianca's gaze had been empty, her lips so blue they'd looked black in the mist.

There was no doubt about it.

Bianca Evans – failed actress, bankrupt fashion designer, and daughter of the famous Larry Evans – was dead.

⸻

IF THE MOOD FOLLOWING THE DISCOVERY OF ANNE'S BODY had been uncomfortable, the air in the kitchen after discovering Bianca was devastating. And not because people were crying, but because most showed no emotion at all. DI Ramsbottom might as well have gathered the group to tell them about parking tickets, not the death of one of their own.

"Right, that's the last of you," Ramsbottom said as he waddled into the room behind Scott, who looked even worse for wear without the flattering glow of a fire to warm his sallow, sunken cheeks. "Can we get some heat on in here? It's as cold as a morgue ... if you'll pardon the pun."

DI Ramsbottom pulled the tails of his hunting hat further over his ears, and his thick coat added more bulk to his already boulder-like frame. He gave the dials of the stove a couple of clicks, turning each on.

"The price of gas is—"

"Not now, Kirsty," Mark interrupted. "I'd ask who died and left you in charge, but we all know the answer. Now someone *else* is dead, and you're complaining about gas prices?"

Aside from her own, Mark was the only one who had shed tears over Bianca. Claire had to pull him back into the house, half shivering to death. Together, they'd waited by the fire and watched as the ambulance pulled away. They didn't turn the sirens on, and the police flooded in soon after.

"The early estimate suggests Bianca was in that pond

for at least an hour," Ramsbottom said, holding his hands out to the flames Claire could only smell and not feel. "Which means she likely died around sunset."

The exact time Claire arrived. She regretted her decision to sneak in through the conservatory at the back of the house.

"I was by the fire," Scott said, nodding at Claire. "You can attest to that."

"I did arrive as the sun was setting around an hour ago," Claire stated, without putting any sway on her inflexion. "Scott was by the fire in the library, working on his laptop. I sat with him for a while and then went to Mark's room. I saw Scott enter his room, Kirsty was in her room with the door open, and I heard music coming from Carol's room."

"I've been sculpting in there since you saw me earlier," she explained, holding open her clay-covered hands. "I've only left my room to use the facilities and make dinner. I've been glued to my space heater. From the sounds of it, aside from Scott, we were all in our rooms. Who's to say any of *us* killed her?"

Claire arched a brow. The question of murder or guilt hadn't come up until Carol blurted it out. Carol looked around the table as though hearing the echo, and there was a shifting of eyes just like when Bianca had confronted them about the paintings.

Even now, it felt like they were ignoring Bianca.

"She probably drowned herself," Kirsty said. "Did you check her pockets for stones? Oh, don't look at me like that, Mark."

"Why would Bianca take her own life?"

"We all know what Bianca was like," Kirsty said, scanning the table. "She was an emotional wreck on the best of days. You saw her outburst earlier."

"She was devastated about losing her father's paintings," Claire said. "Have you tracked them down, Detective Inspector?"

"We *are* working on it." Ramsbottom's sigh suggested progress was slow. "She came into the station earlier and made quite the scene, insisting that we weren't taking the matter with the paintings seriously."

"You weren't." The firm words left Claire's mouth before she could swallow them. "And now that she's dead, I think it's time to consider that the Larry Evans paintings – which, as Bianca pointed out, are mostly missing – might be why Anne is dead. Bianca wanted to *find* the paintings to preserve her father's legacy. Why would she take her own life now?"

"Because she was always giving up on things," Kirsty said. "I'll go and turn up the boiler. Em didn't give us a straight answer about lowering the rent, so we need to cut costs if we're going to stay here. I don't have anything else to say. I've been in my room all night, trying to pull this craft fair together."

Claire could hardly believe her ears.

After the deaths of two members of The Collective so close together, Claire couldn't understand why they weren't all sprinting off into the countryside to get as far away from Starfall House as possible. And yet, she didn't get up from the table either. Instead, she stayed put and looked into the eyes of The Collective as each retreated into themselves.

Scott.

Carol.

Kirsty.

Even Mark.

The conservatory door opened, twisting Claire around in her chair. Granny Greta, the last person she expected to see, hurried into the kitchen. Spud, her Yorkshire terrier, pulled in Claire's direction, but Greta's eyes went straight to Ramsbottom.

"I need to report a sighting," she said, catching her breath between each word, "to someone who can grow facial hair. You've got a team of children out there, Harry."

"All fully qualified, I assure you, Mrs Harris."

Ramsbottom pulled out a chair for Greta, and she sank into it, noticing Claire for the first time. She was startled, and then her bony fingers wrapped around Claire's. Spud sprang into Greta's lap and sat with an open-mouthed expression that was the only thing close to a smile in the room.

"A sighting, Gran?"

"Yes, love. I was out walking Spud around sunset. You know how I like to catch the last of the light. Getting earlier and earlier, so I left my house around three. I stopped on the corner to talk to Shelly for a bit and—"

"The sighting, Mrs Harris?" Ramsbottom offered her a digestive from a packet he'd found in the cupboard. "What did you see?"

"Right." Greta caught her breath, and Spud yawned. "I let Spud lead the way, and he took me all over the park today. Loves the snow. Eats the stuff, the silly sausage." She tickled his head. "He was headed toward the duck pond when I saw someone put something white into the pond. I thought they might be trying to get rid of a duvet or something. You know what people are like with fly-tipping around here recently. Someone left a broken washing machine right outside my back gate. Almost broke my neck tripping over the—"

"Do you have a description of who you saw?" Ramsbottom pushed, pen already primed at his pad.

"Yes. They were wearing red."

Claire looked to Carol, as did everyone else in the room. Frowning, Carol squirmed in her seat, tugging her clay-spackled cardigan together.

"That doesn't mean anything," she protested. "It's a

festive colour. I won't be the only person wearing red today."

"No, but it *was* a red cardigan," Greta said, letting go of Claire's hand and tapping the table in Carol's direction. "The fog was starting to roll in, but I could see the red fabric floating behind them as they ran away. I was on my way over to see what they'd left in the pond, but Spud started doing his circling ritual, and being the responsible dog owner I am, I got my bag ready to pick it up and – oh, dear. You don't think … if I'd gone over? Maybe the poor woman might have been alive, and I could have helped her?"

"You can't blame yourself, Gran."

"Yes, no use in that, Mrs. Harris. But I suggest you sit down, Carol." Ramsbottom stretched out a finger, and Carol sank back into her chair. "You were in your room alone, you say?"

Kirsty slipped back in, and with Greta having taken her chair, hovered at the back of the room. Claire felt the first wisps of hot air drifting from the radiator as the pipes creaked to life.

"Yes." Carol forced a laugh, examining the room for an ally. "This is ridiculous. I didn't kill Bianca. What reason would I have?"

"She outed you earlier," Kirsty said. "We all heard her expose that you tried to leech money from Anne, only to be rejected. If that's not a motive for murder, I don't know what is."

A silence followed, and Claire could see the theory taking hold. Given what Greta had seen, it made sense. The crackle of Ramsbottom's police radio broke the silence as he ordered his officers to search Carol's room.

"You cannot do that."

"Got something to hide, Carol?" Mark asked.

"No, but I deserve privacy." Carol's eyes darted around the room like an animal about to start thrashing in its cage. "I haven't done anything. Really, I haven't. I didn't kill Bianca."

Another silence followed.

"So, you admit it?" Kirsty said. "You didn't kill Bianca, but you *did* kill Anne?"

"I didn't say that!"

"Sounded implied, though," Mark added, seemingly on Kirsty's side for the first time since Claire had seen them in the same room. "Like I said, if you have nothing to hide, you have nothing to—"

"Sir?"

A baby-faced officer pushed into the kitchen holding up a plastic bag pinched between two fingers. The bag contained a screwdriver and a dozen or so screws and washers.

"Found this under her mattress," he explained, handing it over to Ramsbottom.

"The table at the craft fair," Claire said, staring at Carol as she shrank back. "You took the screws out."

"That was planted. I've been framed!"

"Carol Poole, I'm arresting you for the murders of Anne and Bianca Evans. You do not have to say anything. But it may harm your defence if you do not mention when questioned something which you later rely on—"

"No." Carol stood up, hands in knots. "You've got it all wrong."

"*Something* which you later rely on in court," Ramsbottom continued, raising his voice as the young officer pulled his cuffs from his belt. "Anything you do or say may be given in evidence."

"No." Carol pushed back against her chair; the legs screeched against the tiles. "This isn't what it looks like. I took the screws out of Anne's table. I admit it, okay? It was a moment of madness, but I didn't *kill* her." She laughed as though the accusation was ludicrous. "I didn't kill *anyone*."

The handcuffs cranked around her wrists, and she wriggled all the way to the back door. Claire recalled Carol coming in through the same back door the afternoon Anne was murdered, fresh from a hike, wearing a pair of walking boots.

"It was *just* the table," Carol's voice echoed around the conservatory as they dragged her out of view. "Just the table!"

CHAPTER TEN

*S*tanding on the path outside Starfall House, Claire counted along the windows from the right-hand side. She knew the corner window led to the bathroom sandwiched between the staircase up to the attic and Carol's room. Mark crouched directly between the second and third windows.

"I found the key *right* here," he said, pausing his squat-shuffling. "Have you got a light on you?"

Claire pulled out her phone and shone the flash down into the snow. Hunkering next to him, she saw the perfect impact of a key and a shooting star.

"We're right below Carol's room," Claire confirmed, looking up. "Does it look like it dropped from above to you?"

"I was thinking the same thing." He glanced up at her

as he pushed himself to his feet. "Stand up but don't move." His finger pointed along the snow. "Those are my footprints from earlier, when I noticed the key glinting in the sun. This trail is mine from now, and that's yours." He looked up. "She must have thrown it out the window?"

"Hardly the best way to get rid of something. Snow's never here to stay."

"I heard it was sticking around till Christmas." Mark reached into his jacket and produced the key. He held it up in his gloved hands. "And why? Why would she throw it out the window? Why would she even have it?"

"Maybe the estate agent gave it to your mum?"

Mark hopped off the grass and onto the path, and Claire joined him. "She told me she didn't have a key for the observatory. And if Carol had it, why is it important?"

"This would be a good time to hand it over to the police."

"It would." He twirled the key around his finger, winking. "We *were* on our way there."

They set off, giving the pond a wide berth as the clinical trappings of a crime scene swallowed it up. Claire wasn't sure she would ever be able to look at it the same way. This turn of events made her own dip seem inconsequential. They walked around the grass, passing the Chinese garden that occupied the left side of the large park.

"Do you think Carol is behind this?" Mark asked,

making Claire notice the silence that had settled as the observatory loomed closer.

"She sounded pretty convincing," Claire said. "But she could have been admitting to the smaller lie to cover up the bigger one. Feels good to know the table didn't fall apart from the sheer force of my backside. I really only tapped the thing."

"Quite an extreme thing for her to do," he said. "I didn't think she was that way inclined, but I never trusted her, especially after I found out she asked my mum for that hundred grand."

"She asked for one hundred thousand pounds? She made it sound like she asked for a *small* loan. And you're right. Sabotaging that table was extreme. She must have wanted to get her own back, yet when I talked to her, she made out like they were practically sisters."

"She likes to push that narrative." Mark rolled his eyes. "After Larry suggested that my mother retire, Carol barely saw her. They were work friends, that's it. Then she got wind that Larry had died and Mum had cashed in. She came to the funeral professing that she would be there for my mum and calling herself my 'Auntie Carol' out of nowhere. It was all so forced, but my mum didn't notice. She never did. I was the only person on *her* side, yet I became her enemy. After hearing that they all tried to poison me against you, it makes a kind of sense that Mum misinterpreted my worries about getting her affairs in order. I'm not surprised Scott or Carol would stoop low enough to suggest I murdered my mother, but Kirsty should have known me better than that."

The path flattened out, and Claire took in the view. In the distance, the Warton Candle Factory lit up the fog on the opposite hill.

Claire realised she hadn't mentioned knowing about the true nature of Mark's relationship with Kirsty – the very reason she'd gone to Mark's room in the first place. If only pictures, keys, and a body in a pond hadn't side-tracked her so completely.

"The two of you were engaged," Claire stated as they lingered by the grand front doors of the observatory. "You never mentioned it."

"No, I didn't." Mark buried his hands in his jacket pockets as he bowed his head. "She told you? I assume she only had lovely things to say about me and made out like it was her decision to call off the engagement?"

"Scott told me. And was it?"

"I was the one who suggested we spend some time apart. I said she could say it was mutual, but she went in the opposite direction and took credit for calling off the engagement. Didn't help the rift with my mother. I gave Kirsty three years, but I couldn't give her any more."

"And yet here you are, together."

"Believe it or not, it wasn't planned." He glanced at her under his brows, but his eyes didn't linger. "I thought she was finished working for my mum. She made this big speech about moving on to 'finally find her success', but she changed her mind at the last moment and came along. I'd already decided I was coming."

"Scott made it sound like you only came to follow Kirsty."

"And why doesn't that surprise me? You don't believe a word he says, do you?" Mark stared off to the glow of the house in the fog. "I'm sure he's the biggest snake of them all. Kirsty called Carol a leech, but it wasn't like she extracted anything from my mother. Carol paid to live here, like we all have. Why do you think Scott's suddenly working every waking hour? My mum bankrolled his lifestyle from the moment they met, but she didn't see it. I *tried* to make her see, but it always ended in an argument."

"Like the one you had the morning of the craft fair?"

Mark looked squarely at her, amused rather than annoyed by the confrontation.

"You don't miss a trick, do you, Claire?"

"Bianca saw Anne leave your room in tears."

"I don't deny it, and I wish it hadn't come to that. It ended up being one of our last interactions. It's been eating me up these last few days." His head dropped. "She confronted me, telling me to back off about the will. I asked where that had come from, and she said she could 'see what I was doing.'" A sad smile lifted his cheeks. "Like

I said, I think the snakes were hissing in her ear. She seemed upset before she came into my room. Just like when she blew up at you, it came from nowhere."

"You think someone got to her before you?"

"My mother and Scott were bickering more than usual in the days before the craft fair. I put it down to stress from the planning, not that my mother was doing much other than puppeteering Kirsty. This entire craft fair was Kirsty's idea. It was the first thing to put a glimmer in her eye after her art career didn't pan out. Larry Evans ruined her."

"How so?"

"When I first met her, she was still full of hope about making her dreams come true. She was different back then. She changed when her big debut didn't make a splash. She lost her sense of fun. Larry dropped her, and he wasn't kind about how he did it. I don't know what my mother saw in the cantankerous old man. After that, Kirsty crawled to Bianca for a job in her boutiques. She'd organised a few of Larry's events in return for his mentoring, so she was good at planning. Bianca seemed to knock out the last of Kirsty's light before firing her. My mum picked up where Bianca left off, and she didn't treat her much better. By the end of our relationship, I don't think Kirsty could stand that I'd had such success selling my company while she was still struggling. The sad part is, I don't think she's picked up a paintbrush in years. She might not have met Larry Evans' high bar, but I enjoyed her work."

Mark surprised Claire by taking her hands in his. He stepped toward her, closing his eyes. "I'm sorry to make things awkward, but after what happened tonight, it's best to remember how short life is. We don't have all the time in the world like we think we do." His grip tightened. "Claire, I didn't tell you about my connection to Kirsty because I thought you were quite wonderful from the moment you crashed into my life with your trolley."

As flattered as Claire was by the revelation, her mind went elsewhere. Kirsty wasn't the only one who'd gone through an artistic dry spell, and Claire had been acting like she had all the time in the world since stepping foot into the park. She had somewhere else to be.

"Judging by your silence, you don't feel the same way." Mark dropped her hands and stepped back. "I'm sorry, I—"

"I have a boyfriend," Claire explained. "I've known him my whole life, and I've loved him just about as long. I'm sorry, Mark."

"No, I'm sorry." He wafted a hand, turning to the door with the key. "Life isn't a Christmas movie, is it? I should have known someone like you would be taken. I hope he knows how lucky he is to have you."

"I hope so too." Claire backed away with an apologetic

smile. "I need to go. I'm supposed to be at his house right now. It completely slipped my mind."

Claire turned and set off before Mark could protest, glad to escape the awkwardness still lingering in the air between them. His confession had blindsided her, but maybe she should have noticed. Sally had always said Claire wouldn't know if a man was flirting with her if her life depended on it. Mark did seem sweet, though she'd seen another side to him. She wanted to believe his version of events, but did the amount in his bank account prove anything?

Crunching through the snow as carefully as she could, Claire paused by the marble fountain where she'd first met Mark. She looked back to the observatory, wondering if he'd gone in alone. There was a chance his declaration of her being 'wonderful' was a bluff to throw her off his scent. If so, he'd been a better actor than Bianca Evans.

Claire checked her phone. No messages from Ryan yet, so she might not be late. It wasn't like he'd given her a specific time.

Music was pumping from Warton Candle Factory on the distant hill opposite, where they were probably having their Christmas party, the Crimbo Bash.

Claire had hoped last year's party would be her last, but then, she'd gone into every new year hoping for the same thing. Somehow, it had happened; this was the year she'd realised her dream of owning her own candle shop. She hadn't been able to foresee how challenging it would be to keep the shop afloat … and she certainly hadn't dreamed that she wouldn't be living the dream alone. Smiling, she set off again. She and Ryan had seen too little of each other in the past few weeks, and she had planned to make up for it, starting now.

A snowball to the temple blindsided her again, albeit more literally. The ice projectile exploded against the side of her head; the splitting pain was immediate and all-consuming. Her hands went up instinctively, even as her feet slipped out from under her. She skidded on the ice beneath the fresh snow and landed with pain to rival the throbbing at the side of her head.

"Ow," Claire moaned to herself as she stumbled to her feet. "Who threw that?"

Blinking back tears, she squinted through lenses speckled with melting snow. She pulled off her glasses and rubbed them against her sleeve. Things were blurry, but she'd be able to see movement. It would be less frightening than the reality, which was the still silence. The snowball had come as if from nowhere.

As she put on her glasses again, her fingers brushed against something warm on the side of her head.

"Oh, fantastic." She looked down at the blood on her hand, then to a lump of black coal sitting in the snow. "That's just unfair."

LATER THAT EVENING, THE DOCTOR CLIPPED AN X-RAY against a lightbox in a private room at Royal Blackburn Hospital. "Nothing seems to be broken. You're lucky to be walking away from this nasty fall with only a bruise."

"A *bruise?*" Janet exclaimed from the chair next to Claire's bed. "I saw her backside. It was black and blue."

"The x-ray doesn't lie, Mum," Claire said, wincing and wondering when the painkillers would kick in. "I'll be fine. Feeling better already."

"Honestly, Claire, you've always been so accident-prone."

"Hang on, dear," Alan said, leaning forward in his chair on the other side of the bed. "Claire only fell over because someone threw a lump of coal wrapped in snow at her."

"And you all wonder why I hate this time of year. Preposterous that this would happen to my daughter. Throwing snowballs should be illegal."

"Assault *is* illegal," Alan said, resting his hand on Claire's hand. "Are you sure you didn't see who threw it?"

"It all happened so fast, and I had snow on my glasses. I didn't see anything." Claire thought back to the silent park and shivered despite the warmth of the hospital room. "It was probably just some kid."

"They get more feral with every generation," Janet

said, to which the doctor chuckled. "Who wants hot chocolates from the vending machine?"

"I'll pass," Claire said, still scarred from the disaster she'd been served at the police station. "My stomach feels a little funny, actually."

"That'll be the painkillers kicking in," the doctor said, ripping a green sheet from the pad she'd been scribbling in. "A prescription to get you through the next few days. Stay off your feet and lie on your front as much as possible. You need to rest. But other than that, you'll be free to go home in a few hours."

"Hours?" Claire pushed up out of bed. "I have somewhere to be. I should be at Ryan's."

"You're lightly concussed, Miss Harris," she said with a tight smile. "We need to keep you under observation a little longer."

"Then we'll need more than hot chocolate," Janet said, digging in her handbag for her purse. "I knew I should have brought a book."

The doctor followed Janet out, and Claire tried to settle into the bed the best she could. She could still feel the sharp pain at the centre of the bruise, but whatever they'd given her made her not care about it quite so much. If only the ringing in the side of her head would subside.

"Quite poetic that it was a lump of coal," Claire said. "Merry Christmas to me."

"Do you really think it was a random child?"

"I'm not sure," she confessed, her eyes closing as her skin started to warm, as though she'd slippped into a warm bath. "But if it wasn't, I received the message loud and clear."

"What message, little one?"

Claire yawned. "I must be close to finding out who the murderer is, and the one person who couldn't have thrown the snowball is the one the police think did it."

"Don't you think Carol is behind this?" he said, his voice growing distant. "Ramsbottom thinks she's close to confessing."

"No," she replied. "Just the ... table."

Claire awoke with a start to a dark room and a familiar scent. Her nostrils wrinkled as she pushed herself up in the bed.

"Candy cane."

"You're awake."

Ryan appeared from the dark, helping Claire's eyes adjust. The warmth with which she'd slipped off to sleep had been replaced with restlessness. She clapped her tongue against the roof of her mouth and the two stuck together.

Ryan grabbed a waiting cup of water and held the

straw at her lips. "They said you'd wake up with a dry mouth. You've been asleep for a few hours. How are you feeling?"

"Better now," Claire said, refreshed by the water. She sat up and noticed the candle on the cupboard beside the bed.

"Thought it would be nice to have something familiar when you woke up."

"Sorry I missed dinner."

"There's still time," he said with a comforting smile and a wink. "We can order pizza when you get back. Your dad went home to feed your cats, and your mum's wandering around this place somewhere. She can't sit still for more than five minutes."

"Sounds like my mother." Claire wriggled herself into a sitting position, grunting through the dull ache around her middle. "How have things been going with Maya?"

The question slipped out quickly. Maybe the painkillers had loosened more than her concern for her pain. Ryan's sigh let her know it hadn't been plain sailing.

"She's staying at the B&B," he said, his eyes darting down. "We went around in circles for a few hours over her reasons for leaving. She didn't say much that wasn't in the letter. Feeling trapped, living a lie, didn't know who she was. Lots of excuses, not a lot of acceptance or responsibility."

Claire wrapped her hand around Ryan's.

"How have the kids taken it?"

"As well as they can," he said, rubbing his brow. "We all sat down this morning and tried to talk through some things, but it was like pulling teeth. Amelia doesn't want anything to do with her, and Hugo's acting like he has no idea who she is. Who can blame them? Their lives have changed so much."

"Do you know how long she plans on sticking around?"

"I can't get a straight answer from her. 'When things are right' is all she keeps saying." Ryan exhaled. "Will's not in the picture. She said they didn't last long once they ran off. It turns out it was easier for them to spend those five years sneaking behind my back. I can't believe I ever called that guy my friend. Or Maya my wife, for that matter. The more she says she felt trapped, the more I realise that I felt the same. I'm sorry. I shouldn't be dumping this on you now. You're in a hospital bed."

"I *want* to know," she said, squeezing his hand. "I asked, didn't I? All I care about is that you're alright. Everything else is just noise."

They shared a quiet smile that Janet interrupted when she walked in, reading the back of the wrapper of a bar of something.

"I thought I was making a healthy choice getting a fruit and nut bar, but I'm sure there's as much sugar in here as chocolate," Janet said, looking up from the label. "Ah, you're awake. Feeling better?"

"Peachy."

"While you're here, Ryan, I've been meaning to ask. Are you and the children coming to Christmas dinner?"

"Don't put him on the spot like that, Mum."

"I'd love to," Ryan answered. "That alright with you, Claire?"

The pills weren't the only thing warming her insides. "More than alright."

"Perfect. We'll have a big family Christmas." Janet bit the last piece of the bar from the wrapper and held up a finger, making them wait while she chewed. Once she swallowed, she asked, "Will Maya still be around?"

"Oh, I – I'm not sure."

"Haven't you asked?"

Claire had just asked the same question, though she hoped she hadn't made it sound quite so much like an inquisition. Her mother had never been the most tactful woman when it came to getting to the bottom of something.

"Have you asked Grandma Moreen if *she's* coming for Christmas?" Claire asked, returning the grenade.

"What was that, love?" Janet asked, suddenly interested in whatever was happening on the other side of the window. "I think that's the doctor. I'll get her to come and give you a last look over so we can get you out of here and into witness protection. Today, it was coal in a snowball. What's next?"

"Piano down the stairs?" Claire suggested. "House from the sky? That giant boulder from *Indiana Jones*?"

Pursing her lips over her apparent desire to laugh, Janet left the room, and Ryan helped Claire swing her legs over the side of the bed. She wasn't sure how long she'd been at the hospital, but for the moment before the dizziness made her sway, it felt nice not to be horizontal.

"You're sleeping at mine tonight," Ryan said. "You need someone to keep an eye on you."

Claire nodded, letting herself fall into Ryan's chest as he wrapped her arms around her. She didn't argue. She didn't want to. As much as she joked now, she hadn't forgotten what she'd said to her father as she'd drifted to sleep.

If the mystery snowball had been a deliberate message, Carol was the only one who couldn't have thrown it, and it had struck too well to be random. She already knew Mark was in the park with her, and Scott or Kirsty could quite easily have been hiding behind a tree.

Carol's denial during her arrest was all Claire had to base her gut instinct on, yet she believed the woman when she'd said she was only responsible for the table.

Claire just had to find a way to prove it … as soon as the dizziness passed.

CHAPTER ELEVEN

*J*ust past eleven, the hospital finally sent Claire on her way home with a pair of crutches and her prescription in a white bag. When Janet pulled up outside Ryan's terraced house after a cautious drive back to Northash, Claire let out a sigh of relief. She'd got there eventually.

"Don't worry about the shop," Janet said, waving through the window of her work van as Ryan helped Claire to the door. "Your father and I have already arranged things with Damon. We're going to get our hands stuck in. I'll make sure your father keeps an eye on the cats. Look after her, Ryan. I'll be checking in."

"Don't worry, Mrs Harris," he called over his shoulder as he pushed the key into the lock. "She won't be lifting a finger."

"Nothing different there then," Janet said. When Claire gave her a look, she laughed. "You're not the only one who can make jokes, dear."

Janet drove off, leaving Ryan to help Claire over the doorstep. She picked up the scent of her black cherry candle burning somewhere in the house.

"She *will* be coming and checking," Claire said, glad to kick off her shoes. "I'll have to call Damon to apologise and remind him that he's still in charge. Knowing just how my mother gets her 'hands stuck in', I'll be going back to a rearranged and redecorated shop."

"Claire!" Amelia rushed from the sitting room and straight to Claire's side. She hovered, like she wasn't sure if she should give her a hug, so Claire held open an arm, the other resting on the crutch. Amelia ducked in and out quickly. "You're alive. We heard someone threw a brick at you."

"Lump of coal," she said, "and I'll be right as rain in the morning."

"How many fingers am I holding up?" Amelia held up two fingers, changed it to three, then to four, and back to two. "Too slow."

"Hi, Claire." Hugo wandered in, a virtual reality headset hanging around his neck. He rubbed his eyes. "Hope it doesn't hurt."

"Can't feel a thing."

"Why are you both still up?" Ryan asked, helping Claire out of her coat. "Did you twist Em's arm?"

"I sent Em home," Maya said, joining them in the doorway. She put her hands on Hugo's shoulders, but he wriggled away and moved to his dad's side. "I said the kids could stay up. They were quite worried about you."

Like when they'd first met, Maya's eyes – now lined in black beneath a heavy coat of mascara on her lashes – didn't waver from Claire.

"There is a lot of crime around here," Maya said, her eyes darting to the stitches. "Nothing like back home."

"We had plenty of crime," Ryan said, hanging up their jackets. "Where'd you get the headset, kid?"

"From me." Maya exhaled with a wide smile. "An early Christmas present."

"We have to share it," Amelia said. Maya muttered something in Spanish that made Amelia yell, "I'm not ungrateful. I did say thank you. It's just a fact!"

Amelia stomped up the stairs, and it didn't take Hugo long to tug off the headset and follow. This time, they didn't linger, and their bedroom doors shut one after the other.

"You can't buy their love, Maya," Ryan said quietly. "They're smart kids. They'll see through it."

"Hmm." Maya reached around the side of the door and picked up a handbag. She slung it over her shoulder and stepped toward Claire with outstretched hands. Still in a daze, Claire reached out and took them. Polished black nails dug into her palms, and a strained smile parted Maya's berry-stained lips. "I hope you're okay. My children are very fond of you. I wanted to say thank you for taking care of my family." The nails dug in deeper, and she nodded. "Thank you."

"You're welcome," was all Claire could muster as she tried to pull her hands back. Maya clung on for a second longer before letting go. "I should probably sit down. Haven't spent this long on my feet all night."

"I won't stay." Maya squeezed between them, facing Ryan. "I'll come and see the children tomorrow. Enjoy the rest of your evening. Both of you."

Claire rubbed her palms as Maya left. The woman didn't look away from Claire until the door shut.

"That feels like progress," Ryan said, patting Claire on the shoulder. "Get your feet up, and I'll order this pizza before everywhere closes."

Claire walked into the living room, staring at the red marks still bright against the skin of her hand. For the second time that evening, Claire got the message loud and clear. The unspoken end of Maya's speech – the part only her eyes had said – was unmistakable.

Thank you, and now leave us alone.

CLAIRE WASN'T RIGHT AS RAIN THE NEXT MORNING, AND the pain peaked the following night before slipping down to something manageable by the middle of the week. She spent most of that time on Ryan's sofa in front of the three-bar fire, drifting in and out of naps while they watched endless Christmas movies and sampled every takeaway within delivery distance. Ryan looked after her like it was his only concern, with the kids as his perfect assistants. If it had only been the four of them for the duration, it would have been the perfect recovery.

"Maya turned up every day for longer and longer," Claire said to Sally across the counter on Thursday, when she finally felt up to a shift at the shop. "I wouldn't have minded if it was for the benefit of getting closer to the kids, but she kept insisting on 'helping' me. Except I'm sure she was trying to kill me."

"Nurse Ratched-style?" Sally asked, popping the lid off one of the salted caramel lattes she'd brought them from Marley's Café. "Poison in your food?"

"It did cross my mind," Claire whispered. "She gave me a hot water bottle with the lid barely screwed on. Would have added burns to the list if I didn't have a blanket pulled up to my chin. And she ripped the pillow from under my head every chance she got to 'fluff' it. And she kept sitting on my feet when they were under the blanket. From her view, I was the one in the way."

"And from yours?"

"The mood changed whenever she turned up," she confessed, taking a sip of the sweet drink. "The kids are blanking her unless she tries hard to get something from them. The moment they're vaguely happy around her, she starts pointing her phone camera at them, which shuts them down again. And Ryan has no patience for being around her, but he keeps saying it's good that she hasn't given up. I know they need to figure things out, but Maya's avoiding the tough questions."

"Sounds like she's hoping that acting like things have gone back to 'normal' will make it happen," Sally suggested. "Paul used to do that after every argument. Half the time, I was glad to move on, but it wasn't real, and something else was always lurking around the corner. Sounds like the kids might be grey rocking her."

"The kids are throwing stones at her?" Janet called from the shop floor, where she'd been scrubbing under the shelves. She hadn't given any hint that she'd been listening to their conversation, but a silent Janet was an eavesdropping Janet. "Surely that'll give her the message."

"Grey rocking is something my therapist told me about," Sally said, checking her watch as she pulled back from the counter. "It's where you're as unresponsive as possible to someone who's hurt you. Gives them nowhere to go. My therapist says that, from the sounds of it, I've been doing it to my mum and Paul for years without realising. Maya's kids could be doing the same. You only get to lose someone's trust once. And speaking of trust, I'm going to be late for a meeting at the café with The Collective's head."

"Kirsty?"

Sally nodded. "She's been putting pressure on Em all week to accept the lowered rent terms, so I'm going in to put my foot down. Any less, and it'll be cheaper for Em to have the place sitting empty. I know Em's your friend, Claire, but she's not in as much a rush to sell as she makes out. She turned down an offer last month."

The news surprised Claire. "From Anne?"

"Some property developer from down south called James Jacobson. Wanted to turn the place into swanky apartments. She declined. Said it wasn't the right fit."

Sally left and Janet carried her basket of cleaning supplies back to the counter. The place had never gleamed so much. Claire was just glad to find her shop in the same configuration as she'd left it. The Christmas tree in her flat hadn't been so lucky.

"You don't have to stay," Claire said. "It's a quiet day, and I'll be fine on my own."

"I don't mind," Janet insisted, holding up a hand. "You shouldn't be on your own right now. I don't care if Ramsbottom thinks this is a closed case now that they've charged Carol. That snowball didn't just fall from the sky." Her mother paused thoughtfully. "After what you just said about Maya, do you think she could be behind it? Sounds like she's trying to worm her way in between you and Ryan."

"It had crossed my mind," Claire admitted, "but I haven't brought it up. Though she's been making things uncomfortable for me, it's all underhand stuff – nothing I can really prove. If I accuse her and I'm wrong, it could start World War Three."

Janet hummed her agreement as she stared off in the direction of Christ Church Square. "What Sally said about the grey stones and the trust. It's true that you can only lose trust once, but people *can* forgive, especially at this time of year. You forgave me."

"You never abandoned me, Mother."

"But I *was* harsh with you about … you." Folding her arms, Janet cleared her throat. "Just like my mother was with me. You had every right to go grey on me, and you didn't. And before you ask, no, I still haven't called her." In a smaller voice, she added, "We haven't talked since that moment in the pub on your birthday. I haven't *wanted* to. Maybe I've grey stoned her?"

"Grey rock," Claire said. "And as mean as Grandma Moreen can be, she always comes for Christmas."

"And her tongue always ends up ruining it somehow. I just wanted things to be perfect this year. I feel like we've both really found ourselves. You with the shop and Ryan, me leaving the post office and starting my business. Christmas is supposed to be the cherry on top."

Claire shifted in her chair, wishing her 'great year' wasn't ending with so much pain in her backside.

"I suppose," Janet said, chewing at her lip, "that for the first time, I'm confident enough to say that I don't *want* my mean old mother here to ruin things."

"What were you saying about forgiveness?"

"Whose side are you on?"

"Yours, always." Claire reached across the counter and patted her mother's hands. "I just don't want you to regret anything. Like you said, it's Christmas."

"I know," Janet said, exhaling. "And I want you to know I'm always on *your* side, dear. No matter what happens. What I was saying about forgiveness. I hope ... I ... no, it doesn't matter."

"Go on."

Janet shook her head and turned away, still looking off toward Ryan's house. In the silence, Claire heard what her mother had almost said. Janet thought there was a chance Ryan might forgive Maya and give their marriage another go. Claire had felt the suggestion when Janet had given her an unexpected nudge in Mark's direction on the morning of the craft fair.

And Claire had been feeling the same worry simmering in the silences when she couldn't bring herself to open up with Damon and Sally after Maya's arrival. She'd feared it since she waved Ryan off at the airport earlier in the month. How could she not? Losing Ryan was her biggest fear precisely because it had already happened once. The day Ryan left Northash eighteen years ago was forever etched in her mind – and maybe he'd taken a dash of her trust with him.

But things were different now.

Weren't they?

"Lunch time," Claire said, sliding off the stool. "Some fresh air will do me good."

"Yes," Janet said, distracting herself by aligning the candles perfectly. "Good idea. I'll watch things here. And whatever you do, don't go to the chippy. Someone needs to tell Damon there are more food groups than chips and crisps. He ran across to the pub every day thinking he'd guessed the Crispmas flavour, and he was wrong every time."

The Crispmas guessing game used to be a tradition for them at the factory, but her mother was right about how different things were this year. After leaving the shop, Claire looked up at the bright winter sun casting the candle factory in shadow. She'd been able to give Damon a job, and despite what Scott had said about their website, he'd been kept more than busy with the increasing number of online orders. She'd watched the Christmas shopping trickle in on her phone from the comfort of Ryan's sofa – when Maya wasn't trying to break her neck or scald her.

Claire set off on account of what had happened the

last time she lingered too long, looking at the factory; the stitches had thankfully started to dissolve, but she glanced around the square all the same. Aside from a few wrapped-up shoppers, she was alone, though she still feared that another projectile could land at any second.

Her days on the sofa with Ryan had lulled her into hoping the snowball had been thrown randomly. She'd been nowhere near Starfall Park since. Though the case had ground to a halt – from her perspective, anyway – she'd been able to think of little else between her naps.

The conclusion she'd come to was that there was every chance Carol had been framed by the same person who'd smeared Claire's candle in blood.

Her father had relayed the information that Carol still hadn't confessed, and even with her red cardigan and walking boots, Claire was convinced she was looking at the culprit's second – and much more successful – stitch-up attempt.

She walked into Marley's Café, and not just because the vegan café was the only food establishment in the village that didn't sell chips.

CLAIRE ORDERED TWO OF MARLEY'S WINTER WARM-UP Special: spiced vegetable soup with sourdough rolls and a side salad. She threw in some of his brownies, too, hoping their veganness would help her mum live a little and partake.

While Claire waited for her food, she positioned herself so she could see Kirsty and Sally reflected in the shiny glass display. She couldn't see Kirsty's face, but Sally's brows were so furrowed that her eleven lines had popped out.

"That woman is impossible," Sally whispered to Claire when she brought her finished cup back to the counter. "Talk about a stick in the mud."

Sally left with a kiss on the cheek and a promise that the two of them would squeeze in a drink before Christmas.

"She's been in here all day," Eugene said, wearing an apron that looked like a rectangle of a Santa costume as he emerged with Claire's tray. "Sips one cup of tea all day and treats the place like her office. How's your back? I heard about the attack. Absolutely dreadful. Oh, here she comes."

Eugene pushed forward a smile, clinging to the counter. Kirsty placed the cup on the counter, and Claire assumed she'd missed her window of opportunity to catch her.

"I'll take a top up," Kirsty said. "And, Claire, if you have a moment, I'd love to talk. I've been meaning to catch you, but I haven't seen you around for a few days."

"She was attacked," Eugene said, stamping a finger

down on the counter to punctuate his point. "And probably by one of your lot. I've spent all week setting the record straight regarding the rumours your art cult has been spreading."

"The Collective," Kirsty corrected. "And those rumours came from Anne, I assure you. I disagreed with her then and I still do now. The police questioned us all about what happened to Claire with the snowball, and none of us saw anything. Aside from Mark, who was in the observatory, the rest of us were in our rooms."

Kirsty returned to her seat. Leaving Eugene to grumble gossip to his husband, Marley, who was distracted reading a book and sipping tea, Claire joined Kirsty in the corner of the café. Printouts of schedules and floorplans covered the table.

"Please, take a seat." Kirsty offered the chair to Claire as though the table really was her office. "I hope you're feeling better."

"I'm vertical, so it's an improvement."

"You'll be able to sit down at the fair tomorrow," she said, pausing her tapping to look up. "You will be attending as a stallholder, won't you?"

"Oh, I hadn't given it—"

"I've kept a table reserved for you all week." Kirsty glanced at Claire's stitches, and her pen drifted up to touch her own forehead in the same place. "Does it hurt?"

"Not so much anymore," Claire said, though her lower

back still screamed a different story. "I'm sure I can manage a stall."

"Excellent." Kirsty gave one firm nod. "Good choice. That means we're officially fully booked up. And we're expecting an even better turn out. Turns out you can get a lot done when someone isn't holding you back with their old-fashioned ways." Kirsty tilted the tablet and started writing something down on the glass with a digital pen. "I can't believe she had me doing everything on a clipboard, like we were cavemen."

"You said something similar when we first talked after Anne died," Claire remembered aloud. "About Anne holding the fair back. I'm going to guess it was more than a clipboard?"

"It was her entire approach," Kirsty said, sighing and finally locking the tablet. She gazed out the window. "She always thought she knew best. For one thing, she insisted that we use Scott as a designer for everything, even though he isn't very good. I whipped up better flyers in an afternoon than the stuff it took him weeks to finish, and the booking system he put together had so many bugs. That's why he and Anne were so well suited. She thought she could do everything too. Do you have any idea how many different crafts she hopped between?"

"I heard she didn't make anything she sold on her stall."

Kirsty glanced around the quiet café and shrugged.

"It's true. There's no point denying it. She had me do all the ordering. After she married Larry, she kept trying to find something vaguely artsy that would stick, but she had no natural talent for anything, and she wasn't willing to put in the time to get there."

"Unlike you," Claire said, glad Kirsty was opening up. "I heard you were a painter. A former Larry Evans protégé."

Kirsty stiffened. "Yes. Ancient history, now. Didn't work out." She started gathering the papers together into a neat pile. "Here and now, I have a chance to make *this* into something, and it *is* working. It's finally working." The paper and tablet went into a bag, and the bag over her shoulder. She stood, and while holding the chair, leaned in and said, "For what it's worth, I think you were right about Anne rejecting your application for a stall because she didn't want the competition. She sent me down to your shop to get samples. She couldn't hide how jealous she was."

"I'll take the compliment, though I wish I'd kept that theory to myself."

"Tomorrow will go off without a hitch, I assure you," Kirsty said, tugging open the door. "I'll see you then, and I'll make sure you're not behind a column this time."

THE QUIETNESS OF THE AFTERNOON GAVE CLAIRE PLENTY of time to shuffle around the shop, plucking out candles for the fair. By sunset, she had a stack by the back door and a promise from her mother that she'd take them in the van to save her from another trolley incident.

"I'm sure he put it on wonky," Janet said as she stared through the window in the door, pausing her final sweep of the day. "And there's tons of air bubbles."

"What are you talking about?"

"The logo on my van," she said, stepping aside so Claire could join her on the doormat. "It's been parked outside all day. Didn't you notice it?"

The logo with the mismatching halo and wings was plastered to the side of the van, and it did look a little wonky. It still came across as 'jolly funeral home' to Claire, but at least the words 'cleaning service' had been added underneath.

"Cost me another three hundred just to add those words," Janet said as though reading Claire's mind. "You were right, though; they do make the difference."

Claire blinked at her mother. "*Another* three hundred? How much did you pay for the logo in the first place.?"

"Twelve hundred pounds," Janet said, glancing at Claire. "Is that too much?"

"Triple what I paid for mine and, no offence, Mother, but I don't think it's worth that much. You had it done with Scott's company, Northash Design Agency, didn't you? He tried to sell me a website."

Janet shook her head. "Scott?"

"Anne's boyfriend."

"I deal with Ben. A Scottish fella."

"Oh. Maybe there's … more of them."

Claire thought back to her conversation with Scott by the fire. He'd repeated 'Janet's Angels' over and over as though recalling it from memory before admitting that he'd done the work.

"Have you ever met Ben?"

"It's all done over the phone." Janet moved away from the door, still sweeping. "Now, let's get this place closed for the day. Are you coming to the cul-de-sac for cottage pie?"

Claire declined, wanting to spend the night in her flat with the cats after spending so many days on Ryan's sofa. Janet whizzed around to do another round of jar-position-tweaking to make the shiny labels face out perfectly – something Claire had done a lot more of when she first opened – and left with a promise that they'd see each other in the morning.

After picking up the Christmas tree and reattaching the fallen baubles, Claire fed the cats – who she wasn't quite prepared to turn into slippers just yet, despite their antics – and settled into her own sofa with a coffee.

No sooner had she sat down than she sprang back up again.

Scott had said he designed Janet's logo, but he'd also revealed another connection to Claire during that conversation. He'd lodged with her Granny Greta.

Greta had been taking in lodgers to tide her over since Claire's grandfather had died. It wasn't even strange that Greta hadn't mentioned Scott. Her lodgers often came and went in short order – barely a part of Greta's life, let alone Claire's.

What forced Claire out of her chair was remembering that she'd *seen* Greta and Scott together. They'd sat together at the table in Starfall House's kitchen after Mark pulled Bianca from the pond ... and neither had acknowledged the other. Her gran had been overwhelmed by her experience, certainly, but she'd never have ignored a former lodger.

Claire dashed out of her shop and across the square. She passed Marley's Café, one of the few businesses still open, and carried on toward the terraced houses across the street. Greta and Spud were already out, wandering on the edge of the forest behind Gary's Mechanics at the bottom of the street.

"Let's have a look at it," Greta said after greeting her with a hug, spinning Claire around and pulling up her coat. "Well, you've gone from a bruised plum to looking like a woman with jaundice who I used to know."

"Success, I'd say." Claire looped her arm through her gran's and joined her as she and Spud headed toward the canal. "Do you have a lodger at the moment, Gran?"

"No. Are you moving out of your flat?"

"Nothing like that."

"Good, because if you're to move anywhere, it's into Ryan's," Greta said – though it sounded more like an order. "Or him into yours. Or maybe somewhere new together. Does Damon need somewhere? I heard Marley nudged up the rent."

"It's about someone who *used* to lodge with you. Sometime over the summer. A man called Scott?"

"Scott who?"

"Scott Harper."

"I don't know any Scott." Greta shook her head. "I only had one lodger over the summer. A man called Ben."

"Ben?" The name pricked up Claire's ear for a second time. "Scottish fella?"

"That's right. If you know him, tell him he still owes me rent for that final week, and I haven't forgotten about it."

Greta pulled away to attend to Spud's business, leaving Claire to stare into the partially frozen surface of the canal. Who was Scottish Ben, and why had Scott told her he'd lodged with Greta? He'd even mentioned Gary's Mechanics.

"This Ben," Claire asked as they took the path down

the side of the pub – it sounded busy from the chatter and laughter. "What did he look like?"

"Great big bushy beard," she said, motioning at her face, a black doggy bag swinging from her thumb. "Looked terribly itchy. I think he was homeless before he came to me, which was why I let him off without a deposit, but that doesn't excuse him flitting out on me without paying that final week."

"No," Claire said, distracted. "It doesn't."

They followed Spud in a lap around the clock tower before he took them back down the side street. Eugene and Marley were locking up for the day, whispering between them. Eugene glanced in their direction and let out an almighty gasp.

"Claire, have you heard?" he whispered, tugging the lapels of his double-breasted jacket tight. "Our last few customers were police officers, and they told me—"

"You eavesdropped," Marley corrected.

"Carol's out!" Eugene carried on. "Some people from the factory came forward to confirm her alibi. They saw her leaning against the factory wall, catching her breath and sipping water. They only remembered her because she chastised them for smoking so close to her. Their break logs prove they saw her during the window in which she was meant to have murdered Anne. She was framed!"

"But I *saw* her running away in that red cardigan,"

Greta said, the doggy bag hitting her thigh as her hands motioned by her hips. "I *know* I didn't imagine it."

"You did see it, Gran." Claire was unable to take her eyes from her gran's hand, still hovering by her hips. "Did the cardigan seem particularly long?"

"Well, no." Greta motioned by her middle again, this time more deliberately. "It was a normal-sized cardigan. I could see their legs. That's how I knew they were running."

"Claire?" Eugene urged, clutching her arm. "We once stayed in a B&B run by a psychic who would get that exact look on her face whenever she was having a premonition. What is it?"

Claire wasn't sure she was psychic; she just hadn't been asking the right questions until now.

"I helped Carol into her cardigan once," she said. "She's tiny. The thing spread around her like a cape. You already said it, Eugene. Carol was framed, and like my candle, they used an easy identifier. Carol's been wearing a red cardigan *every* time I've seen her, *except* for when she came back for that walk. She was telling the truth."

"They should still charge her for taking those screws out," Greta said firmly. "She tried to make you look like a fool."

"She loaded the gun for Anne to pull the trigger. I just barged in and pulled it for her. This lodger of yours. Scottish Ben. Was he tall?"

195

Greta measured above her head. "And then some. Stringbean of a fella. Where are you off to, Claire?"

"Starfall Park," she called over her shoulder as she hurried back into the square. "I need to talk to—"

A glance in the direction of her shop brought her to a skidding halt. She caught herself against the cold stone of the clocktower before she could succumb to the forces of gravity once again.

Amelia was on the doorstep, curled up in the coat of Ryan's Claire had barely squeezed into, a backpack at her feet.

CHAPTER TWELVE

melia kicked her shoes off at the door and dragged her backpack into the spare bedroom. Claire picked up the Christmas tree again but didn't bother scrambling around for the fallen decorations. Domino was fighting with a bauble in the corner, and Sid was on his back under the radiator. In the guest bedroom, Amelia pushed aside the clothes she'd already left there and started unpacking.

"I've run away," Amelia stated, plopping her colouring books and felt tips on the bedside table. "I hate it there." She glanced at the phone in Claire's hands. "Please don't tell my dad where I am."

Claire paused her typing. She didn't want Ryan to worry, but she also didn't want to send Amelia bolting for the door. She rested her phone on the drawers and held her hand up in defeat. Claire remembered something her father had once said about hostage negotiation when her mother wouldn't let her leave the dinner table without eating her vegetables: Always make the person making the demands feel like they're holding the cards, and don't give them anything until they give you something in return. In Claire's case, twisting her mum's arm to have dessert afterward would let her choke down her broccoli.

"You want a hot chocolate, kid?" Claire flicked on the lamp, leaning against the drawers as Amelia stuffed her balled up clothes inside. "Cream and marshmallows?"

"Yes, please." Amelia moved onto the next drawer. "And chocolate sauce?"

"*And* chocolate sauce?" Claire sucked the air through her teeth. "Why don't you tell me what made you want to run away?"

"They're arguing again." Amelia slammed the drawer and hung her empty bag on the back of the door. "That's one. I know this game. Tit for tat. They taught it to us at school. You want the rest of the story? I want ice cream, too."

Claire's mother would have called Amelia 'too smart for her own good' in that moment, but Claire couldn't help but feel impressed by the gutsy ten-year-old. She saw so much of herself at that age in her.

"You're a tough negotiator, but I think I can stretch to ice cream."

While Amelia settled herself on the sofa, Claire quickly sent Ryan a text message letting him know Amelia was with her and she was safe. She waited for Ryan to see the message as the kettle boiled, but it was still on 'delivered' when she joined Amelia on the sofa. Amelia held a book covered in shells on her lap.

"Never got to show you the photo album Hugo and me made for dad," Amelia said, passing the book to Claire in exchange for the hot chocolate. "We asked all our family if they had any pictures of him." A dark look crossed her face. "*She* took all the pictures when she left."

Claire accepted the album and flicked through it. She'd expected more landscape shots like the ones Ryan had spent all week painting, but Ryan was the subject of every photograph. The first pictures surprised her. His freckled skin had an uncomfortable rawness to it, but he still looked like the plump dumpling she'd waved goodbye to eighteen years earlier. Each picture filled in a jigsaw piece of the man he'd been in the years he was away. She couldn't believe she hadn't known him a day in his twenties – but there he was, slightly older, slightly smaller. If the pictures were to be believed, his confidence had grown with each passing year.

"I think it's lovely," Claire said, placing it on the coffee table before splitting the two spoons between them. "You should give it to him for Christmas."

"He already knows we made it. He asked everyone for

pictures too, but of us from when we were babies. *She* took *all* of the pictures."

Another detail Claire hadn't known.

"How'd you sneak out?"

"Drainpipe."

"Amelia." Claire paused, feeling her lips purse and wondering just how closely she resembled her mother at the moment. "That's dangerous."

"Why are adults like that?" Amelia sighed. "I know you used to do the same thing because my dad *told* me you both did, back when you lived next door to each other. It was easy and I'm fine. I'm not a baby."

Claire couldn't argue, especially since she wasn't sure she was in any place to play the role of a responsible adult, but she did feel protective of Amelia, now more than ever.

"One day, when you're as old as your dad and me," Claire said, to which Amelia sulked as though she'd heard it all before, "you'll look back on your life, and you'll realise all of the mistakes you made. Including all those silly times you could have got yourself killed by not thinking things through. I wouldn't slide down a drainpipe today, and not just because I'd probably rip the thing off the wall. Especially not in this weather." She heard her mother's voice too. Softening, she said, "Promise me you won't do it again?"

"Fine."

"Thank you." Claire cracked the lid off the ice cream and held it out for Amelia to rip off the plastic. "I ran away to my Granny Greta's a few times."

"You?" Amelia frowned. "Why?"

"Have you met my mother?"

They shared a laugh and took their first sips of the hot chocolate. It was better than the muck she'd suffered through at the police station and hospital, but she still couldn't get it quite like how her dad made it.

"It'll get easier, you know," Claire said, dragging her spoon across the hard top layer of the chocolate ice cream. "Your parents will always be your parents, but one day, you won't feel like running away from them. Things can get better. And if they don't, you'll have your *own* home, and then *you* get to *choose* if you want to let them in." She held the ice cream still while Amelia dug her spoon in, going for a brownie chunk that took half the top layer with it. "Want to know a secret? Sometimes my front door buzzer rings *really* early on Sunday mornings, and I *know* it's my mother. And I just roll over and pretend I didn't hear a thing."

"Being a grown-up sounds great."

"You'll find out." Claire wasn't going to burst that bubble. Despite the obvious perks, some days, she'd go back in a heartbeat. "Enjoy being a kid, kid. You don't get a second go around to do it all again. At that same time when you're looking back on your life at all the silly things you did, you'll also be wondering where the years went."

"Em says stuff like that all the time. I just want things to go back to how they were before we went on holiday." Amelia's voice shrank, and she said, *"She's* faking when other people are around. Not Em. My … you know. She keeps calling me a baby, and selfish, and ungrateful, and she tells me that I eat too much, and I'm messy, and I'm … I'm …" Amelia's breath sped up and her cheeks flushed.

"You're just trying to live your life?" Claire offered.

Amelia nodded and went back for another dig of her spoon, but she left it jutting out. "I can't leave Hugo. I said I'd go back for him when you agreed to let us move in."

Claire hadn't, but she chose tact instead of pointing this out. "As much as I'd love to have you here, and you're welcome any time you want to run away, don't you think your dad will be worried when he notices both of his children aren't at home?"

"He probably won't notice."

"He most definitely will, and I'm sure the moment he does, he'll be very worried."

Amelia rolled her eyes. "I saw you text him."

Claire sighed and took the opportunity to check her phone. Ryan still hadn't seen the message. She was sure that if he noticed Amelia wasn't in her room, he'd have gone to his phone first.

"You're very observant."

"I saw her unscrew it too." Amelia's heels kicked against the bottom of the sofa. "The hot water bottle. The one that spilled on you. I told her that I saw her, and she said she was tightening it, but I'm not a baby. That's the opposite. I tell her the truth and she hates me for it."

"Some people are like that," Claire said, wondering if she was being too honest while absorbing the shock that the spill *had* been deliberate. "But I'm sure she doesn't hate you. And I *know* your dad doesn't. So, why don't we take this ice cream back to your house, and we can sneak you back in before he's even noticed that you left home in the dark without asking him?"

Like with Claire trying to move into Granny Greta's house, the right combination of guilt and consequences sent Amelia back into the guest room. She packed up her stuff, and with the ice cream in Claire's pocket and their cups of hot chocolate in hand, they walked around the corner to Christ Church Square.

Claire could hear Ryan and Maya from the moment she stepped into the hallway. The downstairs was cast in darkness except for a soft tunnel of light that could only be coming from the cellar.

"Go upstairs and tell Hugo you're back," she said. "Get a film playing. I'll be up there in a minute."

Leaving Amelia kicking off her shoes, Claire crept into the kitchen. They spoke in low agitated voices that the narrow staircase amplified – not that Claire could make out what they were saying. Neither of them sounded happy. Just like the last time Claire heard Ryan speaking Spanish, he sounded defensive.

"She's saying, 'try, try, try,'" Amelia said, her face deep in concentration as she snuck into the kitchen. "And he just said something like, he 'won't go backwards.'"

"Alright," Claire said, scooping an arm around Amelia and guiding her back to the hallway. "Let's go upstairs and—"

"'I love Claire,'" Amelia blurted out. "That's what he just said. He said it again."

Claire closed the door to the kitchen, her heart pounding. Amelia ran halfway up the stairs and leaned across the banister.

"I *know* he loves you," Amelia whispered into Claire's ear. "We asked him, and he told me and Hugo, and he made us promise not to tell you. He said he was waiting for the 'right moment', whatever that means."

"Well, you've just broken your promise," Claire said, not that she could be angry about it. "He really said that?"

"Ugh." Amelia rolled her eyes again. "Why do adults hate the truth?"

Amelia carried her backpack upstairs, and Claire followed, somewhat in a daze. She'd known Ryan loved her, hadn't she? She never doubted that she loved *him*, but it was a topic they hadn't approached. A word they hadn't said, at least not like *that*.

"I've picked *The Lego Movie*," Hugo said, tapping play on the remote for the TV on his bedroom wall.

"Again?" Amelia moaned.

"You *said* I could pick."

"Fine."

"Claire?" Amelia threw herself into a beanbag chair. "Ice cream?"

Claire sat through *The Lego Movie* in a daze, happy to give her spoon to Hugo so the siblings could share the rest of the pint. The film seemed to distract them enough that by the end they were bickering about who was the better character and singing along with the 'Everything is Awesome' song Claire had heard countless times in the background. Even sitting on the bed with her eyes pointed at the screen, she still couldn't say she'd *seen* the movie.

After the credits rolled, Claire coaxed the kids to brush their teeth and change into their pyjamas. After they both promised to stay in their rooms until morning – with an extra warning to Amelia about the drainpipe – Claire crept back downstairs. She'd heard the front door slam at least half an hour earlier, but the kids had been fighting over the toothpaste and hadn't noticed.

Ryan was in the chair by the three-bar fire, his head propped up on his hand. He was fast asleep. Like he had done for her so many nights that week, she pulled a blanket up to his chin. He settled into the chair, barely stirring. She could only imagine how exhausting the last few hours had been.

"I love you too," she whispered, kissing him on the forehead. "Sleep well."

Claire turned off the lamp on her way out and, after listening out for the kids one last time, backed out of the house as quietly as the snowflakes drifting from the sky. All was peaceful in the square until Claire noticed Maya sat on a bench. Her liner and mascara stained her cheeks as she stared ahead. She didn't seem to have noticed it was snowing.

"Don't sit out for too long," Claire said as she passed. "It's going to get even colder." Maya said something in Spanish, and rather than carry on walking, Claire stopped and said, "You know I don't know what you just said."

"I said 'leave me alone'," Maya spat. "I hate you. You stole my family."

Just as she had done during their first meeting, Claire shrank back … but this time, she caught herself. How could she give Amelia advice if she couldn't even stick up for herself?

"I didn't steal anything," Claire said, hands going into her pockets. "*You* left *them*, and they came home. Nothing that has happened since has anything to do with what you and Ryan used to have. I love them."

"*I* love them," Maya growled, standing up. "This place was never my children's home."

"But it is now," Claire said. "Love is something you do, not something you say." She lifted her chin defiantly. "Amelia doesn't like being called a baby, and you can't buy Hugo's love with game consoles. That's not what they need from you right now."

"Are you trying to tell me how to raise my children?"

"I'm telling you some facts." Pushing her hands deeper into her pockets, Claire turned away and added, "They need an *apology*, Maya. But not right now. Get yourself to the B&B. You'll only come down with a cold if you sit out here."

Content that she'd said all she wanted – and needed – to say, Claire set off back toward her shop. She heard Maya's shoes crunching in the snow behind her, but they veered off in the direction of the B&B. Moments later, a snowball hit Claire square between the shoulders from that very direction. She stopped, but she decided against turning. Seconds later, the door to the B&B slammed shut.

Rolling her shoulders, Claire let out a disbelieving laugh. She brushed her fingers against the stitches. When she rounded the corner, someone was hunched on her doorstep for the second time that night.

"Ah, I was only going to give it five more minutes," Em said, jumping up and hopping from foot to foot. "The lock on my boat froze over. Can I borrow a cup of hot water, neighbour?"

"I can do you one better and you can have the guest room," Claire said as Em followed her into the shop. "Though you're lucky, it almost went to a runaway."

"I'M GOING TO NEED TO SUPERGLUE THE THING TO THE carpet," Claire said as she picked up the Christmas tree once again. "Slippers, scarves, and a pair of gloves, Domino. I know it's you."

Domino batted her prize bauble around the kitchen, chasing it like she'd found the fattest mouse in the alley. Em kicked it the opposite way, sending Domino scuttling into the sitting room. Sid yawned but didn't get up from the cushion on which he was perfectly curled in the middle. While Em made their chamomile tea, Claire filled her in on the events of the evening.

"That poor girl," Em said as the two of them curled up where Claire had sat with Amelia hours earlier. Midnight was creeping closer, as was the sleep clawing behind Claire's eyes. "I know they're both going through it, but you know what mothers and their daughters can be like. Amelia must be so painfully aware of everything she's going through, while not being able to fully understand it. I haven't met a single adult who isn't scarred by something from their childhood, but even though divorce and abandonment are common wounds, it doesn't make it any easier. And to think that Maya threw that snowball."

"She threw *a* snowball," Claire corrected. "She could have been inspired. As we learned with the candle at the crime scene, sometimes things aren't as they seem."

"And sometimes they are." Em took a sip of her tea and hummed appreciatively. "I try not to judge people, Claire, but Maya hasn't shown me that she's any different than what I was expecting. I've been helping Ryan with childcare all year, and like you, I've grown to love them like they're my own flesh and blood. They've opened up to me about their mother, about how absent she was. That's not the word they used, but that's the impression I've drawn. The shock of her leaving unbalanced them, but until their 'holiday', I was proud of how far they'd come." She shook her head. "Since her arrival, they've retreated to being those shaken children I remember from when I first met them." Her body sank deeper into the cushions, as though she could feel the weight of the situation forcing her down. "But, whatever happens, Maya must realise that she can only fit into the picture as it *is*, not as it *was* or as she *wants* it to be. She needs to let go so that she can move on. It's the only way she'll ever be there for her children how they need her to be."

"Where were you when I was trying to talk to Amelia

earlier?" Claire said with a soft laugh. "I can feel them looking up to me, like I know how to lead the way, but I don't have any idea what I'm doing. What do I know about being a parent?"

"You're already doing it." Em nudged her, brows arched high, her smile knowing. "It's *The Lego Movie* and ice cream at the end of a bad day. It's also picking up the Christmas tree, knowing they'll knock it over again, but choosing not to direct that frustration at them."

"Didn't you hear my threat to turn them into accessories?"

"Which you delivered so softly it was as though you were talking to a sleeping baby." Em winked. "Like I said, I see the children a lot, and I think they might tell me just about everything. They're refreshingly honest."

"It's because they trust you."

"As they do you, so just carry on exactly as you are, Claire. With you and Ryan in their lives, I'm hopeful they'll get through this. Like I said, these things have a way of working themselves out. Whether that's now or twenty years from now in a therapist's office, it *will* be worked out. There's only so much you can do to help them in the here and now, and you're doing it."

"In that case, I think the here and now calls for an early night. I have a busy weekend of candle-selling ahead of me, and it starts tomorrow."

"I *did* have something to tell you," Em said, sipping her

tea. "But I think it'll keep you awake, so it can wait till morning."

Claire stopped her shuffle to the edge of the sofa. "You can't leave it hanging there."

"I've been wanting to tell you for a few days," Em said. "It can wait till morning, but … Oh, just promise me you're won't jump up and do something right now?"

"I promise," Claire said through a yawn.

"The paintings have been found."

Em quickly put the cup on the table and bounced into a cross-legged position on the sofa, and Claire braced herself.

"I really was itching to tell you," she said, "but I didn't want to say anything that might make you try to get off the sofa while you were healing. Your leg is tapping right now. I know you'd have gone straight there."

Claire rested her hand on her knee. "Fair enough. I was on my way there earlier, but I got side-tracked. Where were they?"

"Sally gave me the plans for the house, and I've been poring over them all week. My family must have had a lot of secrets because the place is full of hiding places. Secret compartments, panels that slide away, trick floorboards. I found some old coins, cigars, and dusty bottles of hundred-year-old vintage whisky that could raise the dead … all of which, I think, now technically belongs to me?" Em considered the point for a second. "Alas, no paintings. So I took the plans back to Sally and asked if she had any others, which she did. Remember the story of my great-great-grandfather building the observatory?"

"The star searcher looking for his lost love."

"He did more than build the observatory. He also built a tunnel that runs up the hill from the house. You should see the thing. It seems to go on forever. Sally said there were tunnels all under Northash, but this is the more modern of the ones she's seen. It's rather spectacular. Now we know how the paintings vanished. There's an old manual service lift running from the attic to the cellar. That's how the thief moved them without detection."

"Have you shown the police?"

"I took the plans *straight* to the police, but they'd already found the tunnel from the other end. It turns out Mark had already found the paintings in the observatory. He said he spent hours knocking for secret panels, and he found a trap door leading to a cellar the same night you were snowballed."

"The paintings were found days ago?" Claire thought aloud. "Why isn't everyone talking about it?"

"Ramsbottom asked me to keep quiet about it," Em whispered. "I assume he asked Mark to do the same. They rigged the place with cameras to try and catch whoever moved them, on the chance they go back."

"Clever." Claire nodded. "Catch the thief, catch the

killer. Like I said, I was on my way to Starfall House earlier, but I didn't quite get there." She paused. "I don't suppose you know of a Scottish guy called Ben?"

Em shook her head.

"Worth a shot," she asked, plucking up her tea and padding across the flat in the direction of her bedroom. She paused at the front door and pulled the safety chain across. "What about Scott, Anne's boyfriend? You said you saw him sleeping on a bench and that he was difficult to recognise because he had facial hair. How would you describe his beard?"

"Big?"

"Bushy?"

"Definitely bushy." Em nodded, standing and stretching out above her head. "Is it relevant?"

Claire wasn't sure where Scottish Ben and Scott fit into the picture, but she was sure she held all the pieces of the puzzle. With the best friend and stepdaughter out of the frame, Claire's lens narrowed to the remaining three members of The Collective.

The assistant.

The son.

The boyfriend.

"We'll find out tomorrow at the craft fair relaunch," Claire said with a shrug. "I'm sure it's going to be an interesting day."

CHAPTER THIRTEEN

rom the moment Claire arrived at Starfall Park the next morning, she had a feeling this weekend would go very differently than the previous one. A-boards advertising the fair lined the outside of the park, with arrows pointing at the house all along the paths. A large 'NORTHASH CRAFT FAIR HERE THIS WEEKEND!' banner flapped above the conservatory in the morning breeze. The paths had been scraped clear, too, with the night's fresh snow piled on either side in two tunnelling mounds. For the first time since the cold snap had begun, Claire was able to walk up the steep path, and she wasn't the only one. The fair wasn't to start for another thirty minutes, but people were pouring into the park from every gate.

"You're going to have a busy weekend," Damon said,

resting the box filled with candles on the marble fountain as they caught their breath. "Will you be alright on your own?"

"My mum and dad said they'd be here before lunchtime," Claire said. "She sent me a text this morning saying there was an emergency and she couldn't help me get the candles here. When I called the house, my dad said there wasn't an emergency. She's glued to the computer, apparently."

"I wouldn't know the feeling." Damon pushed up his glasses, his tired eyes hinting at a late *Dawn Ship 2* night. "C'mon. One more trip and that's all of them. Don't want to be late."

"No, I don't," Claire said, looking to the house. "Today's going to be very interesting."

"Do you know something I don't? You keep making cryptic allusions."

"Do I?"

"You've said today is going to be 'interesting' six times. You're seconds from putting your little finger at your mouth and letting out an evil cackle. What've you got planned, mate?"

"Nothing," Claire said. "I'm just going to see how the day turns out, that's all. You know how much I love crafts."

"Crafts and corpses."

Whether from luck of the draw or Kirsty's idea of

dramatic irony, Claire's new spot at the fair was in the entrance hall, in the space once occupied by Anne's stall of China-bought 'crafts'. Claire shook the table, checking all the screws were present and correct, before setting up.

The stall Anne had picked for herself really was the perfect spot for footfall. Claire sold four candles before she'd finished setting up, and as the rest of the stallholders rushed to finish getting their displays ready. She'd had a little more preparation this time, so Claire had brought along some elements from her old window displays to jazz things up. Plastic black cherries, caramel-drizzled apples, and of course, her trusty crates.

While Claire sold her fifth candle of the morning to a woman who'd come specially from three towns over to catch the fair early – she looked over at Kirsty, who was standing at the top of the staircase with her tablet in the crook of her arm. From the pleased look on her face and the power in her pose, she was reciting Mufasa's 'everything the light touches is ours' speech from *The Lion King* to herself, especially now that she didn't have to share the glory.

The prideful look drained away when the door behind her opened and Carol emerged with a clattering box of clay sculptures. After Carol's days at the station, she seemed to have shrunk even more, and that diminishment only continued as she spoke with Kirsty in hushed tones. From Claire's perspective at the bottom of the stairs, the height difference between the two was more apparent than ever. If Carol was sat on a twin's shoulders with a red cardigan hiding one of them, she still wouldn't quite be able to look Kirsty in the eyes.

Scott left his room, passing the bickering women without much attention. Claire had spent the little time she'd had awake in bed the night before thinking about where Scott and Ben fit into things, and twins had popped into her mind then too. She'd fallen asleep to the sound of Em rhythmically chanting through her bedtime meditation in the room next door.

Mark was about as well. His stall was still in the library, and he'd avoided looking at her the two times she'd seen him so far. She'd wondered if he hadn't seen her as he crossed from the library to the kitchen, but when he made the same trip back with a cup of coffee, he glanced at the candles on Claire's stall. His eyes had gone no further, and his footsteps sped up.

"Claire!" Janet exclaimed as she hurried through the foot doors, dancing around the flow of shoppers making their way in. "You made it."

"What was the emergency?"

"Research." Janet slapped a thick paper file on the top of the candle lids, making a man rip his fingers away from a vanilla jar he'd been about to pick up. "Nobody scams Janet Harris and gets … away … with it …" She panted for breath between each word before dragging off her scarf. "Had to walk all the way here. Van wouldn't start this morning, which is *all* we need. I left your father hobbling behind, and he's picking up breakfast from … the … café …" She clutched her side. "I thought I was fitter than this."

"Even you aren't immune to stitch, Mother," Claire said, though her eyes had drifted to the top of the stairs again. Carol was on the top step with her box, looking like a child waiting to be picked up at a train station. "Catch your breath and watch the stall. I'll make you a cup of tea."

Claire set off in the direction of the kitchen, but she pivoted at the bottom of the stairs. She ducked under the string blocking it off to the public and crept to the top.

"No stall for me," Carol said, offering a weak smile, "apparently, I shouldn't have expected one given that they all thought I was a murderer. *Me*! A murderer?"

"It certainly did look that way for a minute," Claire said with a supportive smile. "Looks like we were both framed at the hands of the same person."

"My walking boots didn't even match the sample from your candle," she said in a lower voice. "But they still didn't release me until those candle factory workers came forward after reading about me in the paper. Thank goodness I've been staunchly anti-smoking since the eighties. I might still be rotting in that cell, waiting for my trial, thinking nobody would ever … would ever believe me …"

Claire pulled the packet of tissues – for wintery runny noses – from her pocket and offered one to Carol. She plucked a tissue out, but not before a couple of drops landed on the sculptures in the box.

"Share my stall," Claire offered. "You've clearly put a lot of blood, sweat, *and* tears into your work. You deserve the chance for people to take a piece of you home as much as the rest of us."

"Share?" Carol's crying stopped. "You think Kirsty would allow that?"

"Do you care what Kirsty thinks?"

A wicked smile took over Carol's face, and she shook her head.

"That know-it-all was quick to jump on my case at the first sign of doubt," Carol said, back to whispering. "And yours, for that matter. I dread to think who'll be accused next."

Claire followed Carol's eye line back to Kirsty, now striding about the fair floor, going from stall to stall. She didn't pass one without making a comment, and despite the smile she wore as she delivered whatever she was saying, very few were returned.

"I know what I did was petty," Carol said, standing up with her sculptures. "Foolish. Childish. But I was hurt … *really* hurt. The money I asked for would have been a drop in the ocean compared to what she had. All those years we were friends counted for nothing."

Carol set off down the stairs, and Claire thought back to what Mark had told her about his perspective on Carol and his mother's friendship. If she came into an inheritance like Anne had, Claire didn't think she'd refuse a request for money from Damon or Sally, but she also knew they wouldn't feel entitled to a slice. And they certainly wouldn't take revenge on her for refusing.

But, like Carol had protested at the top of her voice, she hadn't killed Anne – she'd only taken the screws from the table.

Claire followed Carol back to the stall and packed away half the candles she'd put out, making room for the clay sculptures. Janet's nose wrinkled at the twisted sight of them, a brow drifting up, but she showed restraint and didn't comment. Carol's pride in her work echoed Kirsty's as she put the statues out.

"Claire," Janet whispered, waving the folder. "Aren't you interested in my research?"

"Right. Your scam. What is it? Out-of-date coupons? Please tell me you haven't been clicking dodgy links again. You must have downloaded every virus on the web by now."

"Nothing like that, dear, though 'virus' is the right word for it." Janet slapped the folder down on the candles again, this time opening it. She'd well and truly caught her breath. "Some people go around spreading their rot, and Ben from Northash Design Agency is one of them."

"Carol, do you know a Scottish person called Ben?" Claire asked. The other woman shook her head before moving in on the first person to glance at her side of the stall. "What've you found, Mum?"

"After you mentioned that I might have overpaid for my logo, I started digging," she said, rifling through the papers. "First, I started by having a look at who the agency had done work for around here."

"Pub and chippy?"

"Pub, yes," Janet said, nodding. "Chippy, no. He tried to get them to redesign a menu, but they refused, and the cheeky so-and-so did it anyway and took it to them expecting money. The pub's experience was similar to mine. Overpaid, had to wait months. I encouraged them both to complain to the small business commissioner, and I went to do the same. Only I didn't know Ben's surname, so I looked him up on the government Companies House website." She paused to inhale. "There's a lot of public information for every registered business in the country, yours and mine included. Northash Design Agency was registered under a Ben Harper."

"No Scott Harper."

"Not on this one." Janet shuffled the papers and produced more screenshots of the Companies House website, each featuring a different business. "You can check how many companies a person has, so I clicked his name, and it took me here. Ben Harper is a registered director of Northash Design Agency, Clitheroe Design Agency, Preston Design Agency, Blackburn Design Agency, Lancaster Design Agency..." She shuffled to a second page. "Which is where the name Scott Harper popped up. And then a Scott Benjamin, then a Ben Scott. All variations of similar names registered to similar design agencies. And this is where things get fishy."

"Like they weren't already?" Claire scanned the room for Scott and spotted him in the archway to the library, talking with a group of women. They each had one of his business cards in their hands. "What else did you find?"

"These companies are registered, yet they never file their taxes," Janet continued. "They exist for a year, sometimes less, and then a new company pops up. The only question I had was 'why'. I can't imagine how much energy it takes to keep starting over like this."

"Tax evasion?"

"That's what your father thought." Janet plucked out another sheet of paper, this one showing dozens of low-star reviews. "These companies have the worst reputations you've ever seen. It always starts off slow, and then the reviews start piling in, and before you know it, the company is no longer trading and there's a new one in a new place. All the complaints are the same.

Unsolicited work, overcharging, overpromising, under-delivering. I should have known he was fishy when his email popped up from nowhere, but, well, he said he could do so much for me. Before I knew it, I'd already given him my bank details and paid a deposit. I have every mind to sue Ben for misrepresenting himself."

"If his name is Ben at all."

"Here." Janet pulled out a full-colour print-off of a professional-looking headshot. "This picture was on one of the websites under the name Ben Scott. I have no idea if that's really him because I've never actually seen him."

"That's Scott," Carol said, and they both turned. She was between them, looking over their shoulder. "What you just said, that can't be right. Scott's a good guy. He's lovely, he's romantic, he—"

"Carol?" Kirsty made the three of them jump, and Janet slapped the file shut. "What are you doing? There's no stall-sharing. I told you, we're full."

"Not even for a member of The Collective?" Claire asked, matching Kirsty's volume. "I don't mind sharing, and neither does Carol."

"That's right, Kirsty." Carol gave a firm nod. "My work deserves to be seen."

"Hmm." Kirsty's eyes glazed over the statues before going back to her tablet. "Whatever. Fine. I don't have time for this. The marching band should be arriving soon…"

Kirsty drifted off and Carol and Janet's attention went to serving the customers who'd been patiently waiting. Claire, on the other hand, couldn't focus on candles and clay.

Her mind was firmly on Scott.

Or was he Ben?

Whoever he was had moved on from the library archway. Promising to fetch her mother that cup of tea, Claire left the stall with the file. She went from room to room, scanning for a tall, slender man, but the web designer with the dodgy past didn't jump out at her.

"Haven't seen you all week." Claire spun around to see Mark, his cheeks forced into a plump smile that his eyes didn't quite agree with. "Have you been avoiding me?"

"I was avoiding being upright," Claire said, pointing to the stitches on her forehead. "A lump of coal to the skull will do that."

"I heard about that. I would have come to check on you, but I heard your boyfriend was looking after you, and..." Mark's voice trailed off and he sighed. Quieter, he said, "I'm sorry about the other night, Claire. Really, I am. I wasn't thinking straight. I had this voice saying 'Shoot your shot, Mark. Now or never', and I should have chosen 'never' because of course you have a boyfriend."

"Considering how many years I spent single, could you say that again next time you're around my mother?" Claire asked, and Mark's laugh brought some relief to the tension. "Mark, I'm sorry. I shouldn't have run off like I did. I might not have almost broken my tailbone in the process." Claire wasn't sure of what she was trying to say. "You found the paintings?"

"You know about that?"

"Em told me. I'm guessing the culprit hasn't been back since?"

"Not according to the police. Have you seen the tunnel? It's quite something."

THE SOUND OF THE MARKET ABOVE WAS NOTHING MORE than a distant chatter, but even if Claire could hear them all screaming at the top of their lungs, she wasn't sure she'd have paid them much attention.

"I've never seen anything like it."

"Quite something, isn't it?" Mark's camera flashed. "The sort of thing you dream up as a kid."

In the cellar under the house, Claire stared up the staircase that seemingly carried on all the way to the clouds. She'd been in another of Northash's secret tunnels close to her parents' cul-de-sac, though that dank stone passageway with its ceiling of roots and dripping water couldn't compete with the glamour of the secret stairway to the observatory.

The red carpet on the steps was dusty and threadbare,

the brass handrails on either side were in desperate need of polishing, cobwebs had taken over the wood-panelled walls, and most of the circular lights leading the way were flickering or fully blown out. Still, Claire could imagine exactly how it would have looked when it was first built over one hundred years ago. Judging by the number of shots Mark was firing off, he appreciated the beauty too.

"There was a trapdoor in one of the rooms in the observatory," he said, his voice echoing up the staircase. "Found the crates of paintings, and then this."

"And there were no clues as to who took the paintings there?"

"No, and they haven't been back for them. They either know that someone is onto them or they've lost their bottle."

Or they hadn't been back because the person who'd found the paintings was also the one who put them there. Claire wasn't convinced by her own thought, but she couldn't dismiss it, given that Mark had been in the park with her. He could have crept down the path behind her, packing down his snowball surprise all the way.

But she couldn't prove that.

She pulled the file from under her arm and opened it. Sitting on the bottom step – the trip wire was halfway up – she told him everything her mum had discovered during her research while he flicked through the papers. When she finished, he was laughing.

"I *knew* it," he said, shaking his head while looking at the ceiling. "I *told* my mother. I told you. I told him. I was onto him from the moment he turned up. I knew he was playing a game."

Mark had said that in the chippy too. Knowing what she knew now cast that overheard conversation in a different light.

"He must have killed my mother so he could finally make his move and sell the paintings," Mark said, slapping the folder shut and handing it back to Claire. "And then he killed Bianca. Maybe she figured it out?"

"Or she was simply in the way," Claire suggested. "She was the most vocal about wanting the paintings found."

"Have you shown the police?"

"Not yet. This is still fresh. It proves that Scott might be a scammer when it comes to how he runs his business and treats his customers, but it doesn't prove murder. Not yet."

"What will?"

"I'm not sure," Claire admitted. "Maybe the walking boot that crushed the candle? Or—"

The blare of a horn from above cut Claire off as a festive fanfare silenced the chatter.

"That'll be Kirsty's damn marching band," he said, pushing himself up by the knees. "She's treated this fair like it's the last thing she's ever going to do, but to her credit, she has filled up the place. I've already booked two wedding photography gigs, and the day's only just getting started." He gestured to the folder. "What are you going to do about all of this? It paints a conclusive picture to me."

"Whoever's behind the murders has got away with it twice already, framing people in the process." Claire put the file back under her arm as they set off in the direction of the marching band upstairs – given how deep her mother had dug, she was sure the records hadn't been faked. "I need some evidence, and thanks to Kirsty's marching band, I might just have the perfect cover."

THE FAIR GROUND TO A HALT AS THE MARCHING BAND performed in the middle of the grand entrance hall. Kirsty watched on from the foot of the stairs, clutching her hands to her chest in delight.

"It's *very* loud," Janet cried after taking a sip of the tea Claire had finally got her. "It's putting people off shopping."

"It's festive," Claire called back.

"Festively *loud*."

The band played through a few Christmas standards, moving from the entrance hall to the library as 'Come All

Ye Faithful' transitioned into 'Little Drummer Boy'. Kirsty followed behind, as did some of the customers, but Janet wasn't the only one to let out a sigh of relief as the immediacy of the noise shifted its centre.

Claire joined them in their relief when she spotted Scott's head above the crowd. He reached into his inside pocket and passed the soap stall holder a card. From the crushed look on her face as she nodded along to what he was saying, he'd delivered a similar assessment as the one Claire had received along with his card.

Knowing the window of opportunity would only last as long as the band distracted everyone, Claire slipped under the rope again and hurried up the stairs. This time, she didn't stop at the top. She continued down the landing and straight to Scott's room. She twisted the doorknob, offering up a silent prayer, and the door opened inwards.

The curtains were drawn, casting the room in darkness. Claire slapped the wall until her fingers flicked a light switch. The room was the messiest she'd seen in the house. The bed was covered in clothes and paperwork; the floor, empty drinks bottles and takeaway cartons. The greasy smell hanging in the air suggested some still had leftovers inside them. His laptop sat at a desk, flanked by speakers. The screen was lit up on a page of some kind of code language, but it might as well have been written in Spanish. As a whole, the room looked like it belonged to a man who'd given up.

While the brass band played, Claire hurried around the room, shifting things from side to side. She wasn't sure what she was looking for. If not the walking boots, she needed something else that would point to Scott's guilt. She flicked through paperwork and card stock samples. With all the clothes strewn around, the wardrobe was empty aside from a pair of shoes, and they were shiny brogues.

Out of nowhere, a pile of Scott's clothes started beeping. Claire froze, wondering if she'd triggered an alarm. She dug in the pile on the bottom of the bed and tugged a thick wallet from the back of a pair of well-worn jeans. The beeping came from an electronic tag glued to the inside of the leather. She ran her fingers around its smooth edge for an off switch, but she didn't know how to stop the noise. It was low enough that she couldn't imagine anyone would hear it over the band; it sounded like they were moving across the hall toward the sitting room underneath her. She almost tossed the wallet down until she noticed why it was so thick. The slots for cards were filled, as was the inside section usually reserved for money.

Claire tipped the cards out on the bed.

They were all bank cards imprinted with different names.

Scott Harper.

Scott Benjamin.

Scott Benson.

Ben Harper.

Ben Scott.

Ben Benjamin.

Some were in date, some expired, and all were registered with different banks. She returned to the slots and pulled those out too, knowing she was looking for something with a photograph. Her heart skipped a beat as she pulled out a green provisional driving license. It had expired six years ago, but she knew the man in the picture, even behind a bushy beard.

He wasn't called Scott or Ben.

But it *was* him.

The beeping finally stopped, and Claire exhaled. She pulled out her phone to take a picture but the doorknob behind her twisted. She spun, her eyes going to the safety of the wardrobe, but she'd never get there in time. The door opened, and the man she'd known as Scott Harper came in holding a tiny remote control attached to a set of keys.

"How very kind of you to find my wallet," he said, slamming the door behind himself. "Care to explain why you're in my bedroom?"

CHAPTER FOURTEEN

"*I*'ll ask you again." He inhaled slowly, his feet parting to block the door. "Why are you in my room going through my wallet?"

"And I'll ask *you* again." Claire tossed the file to the floor. It cracked open at the spine and enough of the sheets spilled out for him to clench his jaw. "What's your real name?"

"Scott."

Clicking her fingers together in an imitation of him, she mimicked, "Janet's Angels. Janet's Angels. Ah yes, I remember now, but I probably shouldn't say it because her mother knows me as a Scottish man called Ben." Claire dropped the impression. "But you couldn't deny it because I already knew your company had designed the logo."

His jaw clenched tighter, and Claire could hear the cogs spinning. She glanced over her shoulder at the driving license, the only thing with a name that didn't involve Ben or Scott.

"Peter Patton."

Claire was no witch, but the words produced the same result as uttering a magic incantation to break the spell might have done. His expression loosened, and the layer of vulnerability that she'd seen on his face every time she'd previously seen him vanished with it. He still looked gaunt and exhausted, but fear had taken hold of his gaze.

"How long has it been since someone said your name out loud?" she asked. "Are you from Scotland?"

"No, I told the truth about being from near Blackpool way," he said with a croak. "I lived in Scotland for a bit and picked up the accent well enough to mimic it. Helps with the illusion that there's more people working for the company."

"It also stops little old ladies being able to find you when you lodge with them and run away without paying for your final week. You look better without the beard, by the way." Claire glanced to the door, but he'd yet to move out of her path to the room's only exit. "So, Peter. Care to explain?"

"What's to explain?" he said with a shrug. "You clearly

already know my past, which means you know why I'm where I am now."

"Did you love Anne at all?"

"Nope." He shook his head, his tone matter of fact. "Couldn't stand to be near her. But it's amazing what you can ignore for the right price, or should I say, *prize*. That night in The Park Inn, my date didn't stand me up, but I found a better prospect in Anne. Heard her through the bathroom wall, talking to Carol about all the money she had. I'd go as far as to say she was bragging. I knew right then she was the one for me, so I made sure we met. I forgot to mention I spilled my drink on her to get her talking. It didn't take me long to be everything she needed. Women like Anne love people needing them."

"I know she wasn't a saint, but to kill her for some paintings?"

"I didn't kill her," he said, in the same sure tone. "I knew the first person who put all this together would jump to that conclusion, but I didn't kill her. Or Bianca, for that matter, although that did make moving the paintings easier for me. I should have known to stay away from the observatory, given how obsessed Mark has been with getting in the place. It was a shame when Anne 'lost' the key. I took it, knowing it was the perfect place to store the paintings. I just didn't know how to get them there without being seen. The night Anne died, I came out of my room and saw her there, so I took the opportunity presented to me to make the big move. With a murderer on the loose, they'd be blamed for the art theft as well. Bianca had already started to notice I was moving them down to the cellar in the service lift. I went up to the observatory to find the perfect place to hide them, and, like Mark, found the secret cellar and the underground staircase. It was all too perfect. I didn't even need the key anymore."

"The key you lost."

"Like I said, it didn't matter. I'd been networking with buyers, creating a bidding frenzy using Anne's laptop. I'd managed to split the collection between three people. They were going to pay a fortune. Enough that I could have run off into the sunset and never have to worry about coding another website or designing another flyer again."

"If you had focused on that work instead of on scamming people, you might have built something that you didn't need to run from."

"You have *no* idea how competitive this market is," he hissed, pointing at his computer. "How was I supposed to keep up with this new generation of young coders? Using artificial intelligence, they can pull a website out of a hat in the same amount of time it takes me to type in my log-in details. I didn't keep up. Like I said, I got in on the ground. Do you have any idea how exhausted I've been all this time, going through life alone, trying to survive?"

"Always having to move around will do that to you."

"I learned a long time ago that things usually have a way of catching up with you. I should have left when bodies started turning up, but how could I not try?" Peter looked down at the folder detailing his scams, and then to the corner of the room. A duffel bag leaned against the wardrobe. "How can I not try now?"

Peter darted for the bag, and Claire went for the door at the same time, but she was no match for his gangly limbs. Barely exerting himself, he snatched up the bag with one hand while pushing Claire back with the other. She slipped on the papers and fell onto the bed, half rolling backwards over herself from the force.

"I'm sorry, Claire," Peter said as his face disappeared through the gap in the door. "Think what you want of me, but I promise I've never killed anyone. I just wanted her money. She wouldn't marry me, and she wasn't going to leave it to me in a will, so the paintings it had to be. Pity I'll have to make my getaway without them. I really was looking forward to spending the rest of my life on a beach."

The door slammed shut. Pushing herself to her feet, Claire ran at the door as a key rattled on the other side. She twisted the handle, but she was too late.

"Peter, don't leave me in here."

"Sorry, Claire," he repeated, his voice shrinking away. "I need to give myself a fighting chance."

"*Peter!*"

Claire banged down on the wood, the thuds blending in with the brass band, who'd moved back to the centre stage in the entrance hall.

"Hello?" she called out. "Anyone?"

She looked around for another key, but in the mess, it would be like looking for a needle in a haystack. Abandoning the door, she crawled across the cards scattered on the bed and ripped open the curtains to the bright winter sun. She dragged the window up with a grunt, cramming her fingers under the heavy wooden frame until she could push up with her palms.

"Anyone?" she called down to the deserted path.

Claire couldn't believe what she was doing as she pushed her leg through the window and onto the ledge. Clinging onto the frame, she looked around for an easy way down, and groaned at what she found. A drainpipe. But what other choice did she have? She could drop down, but she didn't fancy her chances with another fall so soon after her last one.

Peter was on the run, and according to him, there was still a murderer out there. Shimmying along a ledge that ran all around the middle of the house, Claire kept her body close to the building and her mind on what Peter had just told her. His confession could have been another of his ruses, but she'd found that she'd believed him, which only left her with two options – and they used to be engaged to each other.

Claire reached the windows of Carol's bedroom, where the cast-iron drainpipe ran down the wall. Chips of paint had rusted off in big flakes, and ice shot out of every crack in jagged shards. Pressed hard against Carol's window, she peered in, hoping to see the sculptor back in her room. She wasn't there, but her red cardigan was – one of them. There were several, all seemingly identical.

"Claire?"

She twisted as Ryan and the kids sprinted up the path toward her. Her shoe rolled on a stone, and she slipped on the ice, making her feel weightless for a brief moment. Her phone slid from her pocket and landed in the snow as she snatched hold of the drainpipe. Screaming all the way down as her hands dragged off paint chips and ice, she crashed into Ryan. Splayed out on the grass, she stared up at the house, wondering if she'd even made it at all.

"But you said we weren't allowed to—"

Claire cut Amelia off with a finger to her lips before pushing herself up in the snow. Hugo handed her the fallen phone, and Ryan helped her up to her feet. The indent of the key had gone, but she was sure it had landed in almost the same spot. Maybe Peter had taken the same drainpipe and dropped the key.

"Dare I ask, Claire?" Ryan clutched both her shoulders. "You could have got yourself killed."

"I can assure you, it was an emergency," she said, accepting Ryan's tight hug. "Scott's real name is Peter. He's a conman. He's the one who was trying to steal the paintings. Locked me in his bedroom and did a runner."

"Anne's boyfriend killed her?"

"He claims not," Claire said, exhaling, letting some of the pent-up adrenaline go with it. She ran her hands along Ryan's back, or rather the back of his coat. The same coat she'd barely fit into. "I think I believe him. And, after what I just saw in Carol's room, I think I know how to prove who the murderer is."

AFTER CLAIRE HANDED THE FILE OVER TO DI RAMSBOTTOM and filled him in on Peter's confession, he sent his officers out to search Northash with a promise that they'd find him. Given how many times Peter had relocated to start afresh, and how long he'd gone without detection, she didn't trust their chances.

What she did trust, however, was that she had the answer. The *correct* answer, and it was thanks to Peter. Or, rather, the process of elimination ruling him out of the murder. Taking the motive of the paintings with him also cleared up other things. Though two suspects remained, Claire knew it could only be one of them.

Somehow, she managed to return to her stall and continue with the day. The marching band made way for a softer choir. By sunset, with all the crackling fires lit and the scent of cinnamon and spice in the air, Claire felt the most festive she had all month.

Maybe it was because she knew it was all about to come to an end.

After the last of the shoppers wandered out, Claire sent her parents on their way with her takings, while she stayed behind with what Carol had fetched from her room on Claire's request. A couple of stallholders were still packing up, but she'd lingered long enough that The Collective had collected themselves in the kitchen.

The three that were left, at least.

With two red cardigans slung over her arm, Claire walked in and joined them as Kirsty was topping up Mark's champagne. Carol, the only one aside from Claire who knew what was about to happen, refused a glass.

"To a complete and total success," Kirsty toasted, raising her glass. "I hope you had a good sales day, Claire. You earned it after pinning all this on Scott. Or Peter, if that's his real name."

Claire had let the rumour spread without correcting it. The police had already managed to find time-logged evidence in the coding on his laptop that he'd been where he'd said he was at the times of the murders.

"It's been like a macabre game of pass the parcel," Claire said, clutching the back of the chair without sitting in it. "First I was the murderer, then Carol, and now Peter."

"At least we know he *actually* did it." Kirsty tossed back her champagne and added more. "What's important is, the fair went better than expected, even with the little hiccup of the police searching the place again. No fights, no arguments, no tables collapsing. I think we can all agree it's a sure sign that our future here will be a positive one. To The Collective."

Kirsty was the only one to toast her glass.

"I'd say it would take someone quite *collected* to pull all of this off." Claire slowly dragged out the chair, making her audience of three wince as the legs screeched against the floor. "Someone organised, resourceful. Someone who knows how to think on their feet, to use what they have on hand. Like a candle as a mock murder weapon, or a red cardigan to dump a body."

"Scott – Peter, I mean, was all of those things," Kirsty said with a nod that clearly meant she wanted to draw a line under the conversation.

"Was he?" Mark arched a brow. "He always seemed disorganised to me. Oh, he played the part well enough, but surface-level charm only goes so far."

"Fooled me," Carol said in a small voice, nodding at the cardigans. "Claire?"

"Right, yes." Shaking her head, she tossed one to Kirsty and the other to Mark. "Silly me. Almost forgot why we were here. Put those on, please."

"I'm sorry?" Kirsty laughed.

"The red cardigans," she insisted, leaning back in her chair. "Just try them on. See how they look. Maybe they can be a new uniform of The Collective."

Mark held it up and gave her a sceptical look. "This will never fit me."

"*Try.*"

Mark huffed, but he shoved his arm into the cardigan all the same. The fabric stretched against the width of his arm as he managed to cram it up to his shoulder. His other arm stretched out wide behind his back. Try as he might to complete the pair, the width of the garment wouldn't stretch across him.

"Told you," he said, screwing it up in a stretched-out ball and tossing it on the table. "What's this about?"

"What was it they said about the glove at OJ Simpson's trial?"

"If the glove doesn't fit," Carol said, "you must acquit."

A knock at the back door made Kirsty exhale. She pushed out of her chair and took their champagne glasses to the sink as DI Ramsbottom lumbered in.

"Any of that going spare?" he asked, nodding at the

champagne. Claire nudged the bottle to him, and he took a little swig, followed by a burp. "Only at Christmas. I needed it after how many times I've lapped this park. There's no sign of that slippery fella."

"He'll be long gone by now," Kirsty said, tipping the glasses upside down on the draining board. "If you'll excuse me, there's still a lot of—"

Mark blocked her from going to the door. Despite Kirsty towering over him, Mark was the one with the bigger presence in that moment. The teddy bear had turned grizzly.

"Try the cardigan on," Mark insisted.

"Why?" Again she laughed; Claire thought it sounded more than a little strained.

"Yes, why?" Ramsbottom asked, though Claire was glad he was already blocking the other exit. "It's nowhere near as cold as my last visit." He rocked back on his heels. "I haven't just come to tell you about the lack of news regarding Peter. I do have news, indeed. It's been confirmed that Bianca didn't drown in that pond. They found traces of shampoo and hair dye in her lungs and stomach, suggesting she was drowned in a bath and moved, so we'll have to search everyone's bathrooms as soon as possible."

"I'd suggest starting in Kirsty's room," Claire said. "Are you going to try the cardigan on? I really do think it'll be your colour."

Kirsty's eyes narrowed on Claire as her brows drifted up to her impossibly short fringe. The two women shared an identical smile, without an ounce of friendliness between them. To Claire's surprise, Kirsty jammed her arms into the cardigan, and it fit just as Claire had expected.

"Please stand up, Carol," Claire said, and the sculptor did as she was told. "As you can see, DI Ramsbottom, the red cardigan, which almost reaches the floor on Carol, only comes up to Kirsty's hips, as per my gran's altered witness statement. Kirsty was the one who killed Bianca and took her out to that pond. You were awfully quick to jump to the suggestion of suicide."

"Kirsty?" Mark demanded. "You've never had a problem speaking before. You're not denying any of this. Did you murder my mother?"

"Ah, we have an update there, too," Ramsbottom announced, patting down his jacket for his pad. He pulled it out and flipped a few pages. "We found traces of silver paint where contact was made between Anne and the murder weapon – an object we're still trying to find."

"Silver and flat?" Claire confirmed. Ramsbottom nodded. "Mark, what colour was your mum's laptop?"

"Silver."

"And did you ever find it, Detective Inspector?"

"We're still making enquiries."

Claire should have known better than to trust that the investigation would be plain sailing at the station.

"Kirsty?" Claire pushed her chair back and stood. She was nowhere near Kirsty's height, but she didn't let her eye contact waver. "Did you really want The Collective to be yours *this* badly? Because that's what it's all about, isn't it? You wasted no time carrying on as normal, taking over the reins and moulding this place to match your vision. In fact, you only spent a single day pretending you were doing it in Anne's memory. You even said it was her idea, but Mark told me—"

"It was your idea," he said, shaking his head at her. "It's true, isn't it? You killed my mother. Say it's true."

"Your mother didn't even *like* you, Mark!" Kirsty cried. "She didn't like any of us. Not her son, her friend, her stepdaughter, and especially not her assistant." Bowing her head, she let out a shoulder-heaving laugh. "And the one person she did like was conning her every chance he had. What a stupid woman she was. I knew Scott – or is it Peter – was moving the paintings. He knew Anne never checked her emails. Of course she didn't. Why would she, when she had such a *diligent* assistant, one willing to work for her living expenses alone? I should have killed her long before we came here."

Carol and Ramsbottom gasped, but Claire could only look at Mark. She felt awful for having suspected him, and even worse imagining what *he* must feel, looking at a woman he was once engaged to who had betrayed him and hurt him in every possible way.

"All of this for a club?" Carol said. "You've lost your mind, Kirsty."

"No, *you* lost your mind thinking Anne cared about you enough to share her fortune. The same way *I* was stupid for thinking Larry Evans would share his world with me. Oh, he teased me. Plucked me from my 'silly little college art show' to parade me around his upturned-nose art friends. Pushed me to paint day and night. Day in, day out. It was never good enough. Never right. He put so much pressure on me, throwing that huge debut event. I really thought I stood a chance of landing with an impact, but I didn't sell a single piece of work. They'd seen it all before, apparently. Larry froze me out from that night on. I should have left, but I stayed for what *we* had."

Kirsty reached out for Mark's hands, but he jerked away, banging into the door to avoid touching her. Claire caught the echo of shared pain in their eyes and knew real love had to have once existed between them.

"And then you went to work for his daughter, Bianca," Claire continued, glancing at Ramsbottom as he scribbled down every detail, yet to ask a single question of his own. How far off had his radar been? "You helped build her fashion label."

"Helped?" Kirsty choked. "*I* built it. I had to teach

myself so much to fit her needs, because she wanted someone to do everything. In her stupid little mind, she was a socialite, but her father wouldn't fund her lifestyle. The only way she ever got any money out of him was when it was for the business. The business *I* built! And just like her father, she promised me the world and threw me aside when she didn't want me anymore. Do you know how difficult it was to watch her business fall apart? All my hard work, for nothing. It was like my art opening all over again."

"Two people are dead because some snobs didn't like your paintings?" Mark said.

"*You* wouldn't understand." Kirsty's finger stretched at Mark, and Claire was reminded of being on the receiving end of her accusations. "*You* found success so easily. Point, click, money. Point, click, money."

"It was a little more than that."

"Couldn't you have just let me have this one win?" Screwing up her eyes, Kirsty backed into the kitchen counter. "The Collective was the *one* good thing Larry Evans gave to me. I thought it was genius. It sounded like the perfect opportunity to finally build something that was *mine*. My break. My chance to say 'This is me. This is Kirsty. This is what I can do, what I can offer.' When I suggested the craft fair to Anne, she loved the idea. It's the only reason I came to Starfall. I was ready to move away, find a fresh start somewhere else. I should have, but she said I could do everything my way. I should have known it was yet another too-good-to-be-true promise. She micromanaged everything, ignoring all my experience and *my* passion for my project. It became *her* craft fair. *Her* vision. *Her* Collective."

"What led to her death that night?" Claire asked.

"You really want to know?" Kirsty sighed, staring at Claire from beneath lowered brows. "You. I went to Anne's room to ask her to put a stop to the gossip. She craved the attention, but she couldn't see past it to all the people – the potential customers! – she was driving away. I told her to let me take control, to do things properly, and she fired me on the spot. So I hit her." Kirsty blinked, and a tear tumbled down each cheek. "I picked up her laptop, and I struck her. Only once, but it was enough. I was … I was so angry. So tired of being used and cast aside. I barely even remember moving her body. It all happened so quickly."

"So much for going to the Chinese garden to clear your head," Ramsbottom muttered, his first contribution. "This is all rather shocking."

"I *did* go there to clear my head. My frustration with Anne drove me there all the time. I half expected to come back and find the whole thing was just a horrible twist of my imagination, but there she was – and there you were, Claire." Her lips curled into a smirk. "Right next to that candle I put there for some insurance. I couldn't have planned it better."

"Except it didn't work," Carol cried, standing up. "Like how you tried to frame me. It didn't work, Kirsty. You've lost."

"That's what Bianca said, right before I held her head under the water in the bath. She didn't half pick a time to touch up her roots. Bottle blonde, and yet she had the nerve to call me a fake. A failure. A loser. She was projecting all her worries onto me, just like she used to. She made my life hell, so I put an end to hers. I thought drowning her would drown out that feeling they put in me. Larry, Anne, Bianca. All three of them poisoned my heart, and they all got what they deserved. I dropped to my knees and thanked God the day Larry had that heart attack. I thought I'd finally be free."

"Oh, Kirsty." Mark sighed, shaking his head. "If you did all of this to be free, you'll be sorely disappointed with what happens next."

"Mark?" Kirsty blinked, her arms going out to him. "What have I done, Mark?"

Kirsty collapsed into his arms, sobbing on his shoulder. He wrapped an arm around her and gave her a few pats, but he didn't lean into her embrace.

Softly, Mark said, "Something I never dreamed you were capable of. Oh, Kirsty."

Kirsty backed away from Mark and straight into

Ramsbottom's handcuffs. As they clicked into place, the weight that had been on Claire's shoulders since the moment she discovered her candle at the crime scene lifted.

"Well deduced, Claire." DI Ramsbottom patted her on the shoulder after he passed Kirsty along to two officers in the conservatory. "You really are your father's daughter."

For as long as Claire lived, she'd never forget the scream that had escaped Kirsty's lungs when she turned the lights on that day she'd found Anne. Kirsty had made her feel more than any Larry Evans painting and had given a performance to more than rival anything on Bianca Evans' IMDb page. If only Kirsty had put her skills to good use – there was no denying she'd put on a great craft fair.

CHAPTER FIFTEEN

*C*laire being the one to pin the murders on Kirsty, mixed with the desperation of last-minute holiday shoppers, was the perfect recipe for keeping Claire and Damon busy in the run up to Christmas. By the last flip of the sign on Christmas Eve, Claire was more than ready to put her feet up and soak in the festive cheer, mince pies, and toffee apple cider as another layer of snow blanketed Northash.

Before the relaxation could really begin, Claire had an appointment to attend. She had accepted an invitation from Mark to meet at the observatory. He'd been into the shop several times, and having spent more time talking, Claire was sure she'd found a friend in Mark.

"I'm buying the place!" he announced as he led Claire into the observatory. "Not just this building, but the house too. It's as good as a done deal. As soon as my inheritance comes in, Em and I can sign on the dotted lines. This way, we'll both get what we want out of this place."

The will Mark had been so concerned with finding *had* existed, hidden under the carpet in Peter's room. Though it hadn't been signed by a solicitor, Carol had been its witness, and she was more than happy to vouch that Anne had decided to leave everything to her son.

"Do you think he'll ever show up?"

"Scott?" Mark thought about it, leaning against the gigantic telescope. "I mean Peter. I'll never get used to that. He'll pop up somewhere one day, but I don't think he'll come back here. The leech sucked everything he could out of my mother. Another day or two, and he might have got away with the paintings. Speaking of which, I have your Christmas present here."

"I didn't realise we were gifting."

"It's more of a thank you, on my part." Mark walked around the telescope and returned with a wrapped rectangle. From the bulging edges, Claire imagined a frame hid behind the paper. "Guess what it is?"

"A new lower back? I haven't felt right since that slip."

"Unfortunately not, but it's the next best thing. Your own slice of Larry Evans' legacy. Sell it, donate it to a gallery, hang it on your wall. It's yours to do with as you please."

Resting the frame against her knee, Claire ripped off the shiny red wrapping paper to reveal one of Larry Evans' signature terrifying pieces. She was sure it was the one her father had first showed her in his shed, early in their investigation.

"I'm not sure I can accept this."

"I insist that you do. I have hundreds." He winked. "More than enough for the launch of the Starfall Gallery and Observatory. It's about time this place was put to good use, and Em couldn't be happier with my idea to open it up to the people again."

"Does that mean you're sticking around?"

"I might be popping in now and again," he said with a shrug, "but I might follow Carol back to Oxford. I feel like enjoying a slice of normality for a while. I don't mind being a long-distance owner of this place. I'm not interested in the glory or the prestige, I just want to do what's right. And besides," he leaned in and whispered, "I've never been a fan of Larry's work. Far too morbid for me." His cheeky smile dropped. "We buried my mother and Bianca today. Turns out, I was the last family for both. With Kirsty behind bars, it's just me now, I suppose."

"For *now*," she agreed with a nod, "but take it from someone who's been there, these sorts of things have a way of figuring themselves out."

"Did Em say that to you too?"

"Yes." She laughed. "But maybe it's true. Time and a fresh start are all you need."

"You're right." Mark stared off to the night sky beyond the glass dome above them and exhaled. "Thank you, Claire. Not just for solving this, but for waking me up. Until your trolley crashed into me, I didn't think it would ever be possible for me to move on. Now I know I can."

They hugged and promised they'd see each other in the new year before Claire left Mark in the observatory to play with his new toy. Grateful for her new snow boots – an early Christmas present to herself – Claire carefully left the park without suffering any more ice – or snowball – related incidents.

This year, for once, the snow *had* hung around until Christmas.

THE FOLLOWING AFTERNOON, AS THE SUN DRIFTED FROM the sky behind her parents' house, Claire pushed away her plate. She'd eaten everything aside from a few sprouts, and she was, thankfully, old enough that her mother no longer forced her to eat them.

Not that she'd have been able to; she was fit to bursting.

"Well done, Janet," Greta said, toasting her sherry

glass to the head of the table. "You outdid yourself this year. Delicious."

"I second that." Alan's whisky went up. "Well done, love."

"You helped carve the turkey." Janet gave a modest smile as though she hadn't spent much of the past week planning out every detail of the feast. "Who's ready for pudding?"

A groan circled around the table.

"For once, I'll pass," Claire said, unfastening the top button of her jeans. "That was the best you've made, Mum."

"Amazing what you can do under less stressful conditions." Janet toasted her wine glass to the empty chair next to Granny Greta where Grandma Moreen usually sat. "Washing up time."

"Leave it till later."

"What will we do instead?"

"It's Christmas," Alan said, raising his glass. "I can think of a million and one things."

"Snowball fight!" Amelia cried.

Half the eyes around the table went to Claire and the fading scar that had been left behind now that the stitches had gone.

"How about a Christmas story," Janet said, fiddling with her new pearls – a present from Alan. "Or we can sing carols?"

"I vote snowball fight," Hugo said.

"Me too," Claire added. "I think I'd rather get pelted with another lump of coal than have to sing carols."

"Hear, hear," Greta muttered half under her breath before draining her sherry. "Count me out, won't you? I'm rather comfy where I am."

"Go and wrap up, kids," Ryan said, and they sprinted straight into the hallway. "I'll be out in a second. Don't go far!"

Alan hobbled after them with his cane, as did a sighing Janet. Ryan's hand wrapped around Claire's, and the two of them stayed at the dining table. When the door shut behind them, Granny Greta twitched and then settled as her eyelids fluttered shut.

Ryan leaned in and kissed Claire. "Maya's gone," he whispered into her ear. "And you taste like gravy."

"*You* taste like gravy," she said, pulling her head back. "Are you serious? Maya's gone?"

Ryan nodded, sinking back into the chair. "I haven't told the kids yet. She slipped out last night, her usual style, but she posted this through the letterbox." He dug into his jeans and pulled out a USB memory stick. A label proclaiming 'Feliz Navidad' hung from the end. "I have no idea what it is, and I had nothing at the house I could plug it into. Your parents still have the computer room?"

Leaving Granny Greta drowsing at the dining table, Claire and Ryan snuck upstairs into the box room.

Despite nobody ever coming up here, it hadn't been spared the holiday treatment; Janet hadn't missed an inch with her Christmas decorating.

"My mind's been coming up with the worst possibilities," he said, as he sat in the rustling computer chair wrapped in tinsel. "Here goes nothing."

Ryan plugged the stick into the computer and a window popped up on the screen. The device had three folders. The first was labelled 'Kids', the second 'Ryan', and the third, surprisingly, 'Claire'. She wasn't sure she wanted to know what Maya might have left for her. Ryan double clicked on the 'Kids' folder and let out a relieved breath.

"Their baby pictures," he said, scrolling through the hundreds of thumbnails. "I can't believe it. She took all the memory cards with her when she first left. This is great."

"Yeah, it is," she agreed, kissing him on the top of his head as she leaned over his shoulder. "What about the others?"

Ryan's folder contained a copy of their divorce papers, her part signed. He let out another exhale and laughed up at the ceiling.

"Who would have thought my soon-to-be-ex-wife would give me the best Christmas present this year?" he said, leaning back into Claire. "Not that I don't love the Larry Evans painting you gave me. I was right about my mum having a print. Found it on the wall in a couple of pictures."

"We're not finished yet," she said, tapping the screen. "There's one for me."

Ryan hesitated over the folder before double clicking. The folder contained a single image, to which they had polar reactions. Ryan gasped, but Claire could only laugh at the picture of a lump of coal as her scar tingled.

"I – I don't know what to say," he said.

"There's nothing to say," she said, peering out the window as the kids sprinted around the side of the house and into the back garden. "Mystery solved. She signed the papers. She wants to move on, and so do I. Maya will always be part of your lives. She's the mother of your children."

"But only my wife for a little longer. What now?"

"Well, right now, there's a snowball fight waiting for us."

Ryan deleted the folder with the picture of the coal, and Claire did the same in her mind as they returned to the dining room. She'd wondered if Kirsty was behind the snowball that had knocked her for six, but it hadn't been part of her confession.

"Only me," Em called as she backed into the hallway carrying a box. "You'll never guess what I won."

"Judging by the contents, you guessed the Merry

Crispmas flavour, and Damon will be devastated it wasn't him."

"I did! Nut roast, cranberry, and cauliflower cheese." Em dumped the box on the table, startling Greta from her snooze. Her red Christmas hat fell off. "I must be the luckiest person in Northash. Things keep coming to me, even if I don't want them. I donated the prize money to charity."

"Come with me next time I put the lottery on, and I'll give your head a rub for luck," Greta said, helping herself to a packet and ripping it open. "They smell foul."

"Yes, they are a little," Em admitted with a laugh, her gaze going to the garden. "Are you to tell me we're in here while they're out there having all the fun in the snow? It's time to celebrate! I'm very soon going back to not being a homeowner."

"You might be the only person to ever be happy about that," Greta said, plucking a couple more packets from the box and shuffling into the sitting room. "Count me out. And fetch me a top up, will you, Claire?"

While Ryan and Em joined the kids and her parents in the garden, Claire added another splash of sherry to her gran's glass. Leaving Greta to nod off again, Claire wrapped up warm – but first, she needed the bathroom.

She reached out for the handle with her gloved hand but stopped when she heard her mother's voice on the other side.

"Yes, Mother," Janet said. "Merry Christmas to you too. How have you been?"

Claire lingered for a moment, then pulled away with a content smile. Christmas really was a time for miracles … and snowball fights. She ran into the back garden, taking a snowball in the gut the second her feet touched the ground.

"You won't catch us," Amelia cried, tossing another ball at Ryan as she ran for the path leading to the front.

Claire tossed a snowball, but it missed by a long margin and went into the garden next door, where Ryan had lived when they were kids. So much time had passed, and yet here they were, stronger than ever. Claire let Ryan toss a snowball in Hugo's direction as he trailed behind Amelia before she pulled him in for a kiss.

"I love you," she said, clutching his collar and staring deep into his eyes. "Just wanted to let you know in case I hadn't already."

"I – I love you too, Claire." He kissed her again, and she felt warm despite the bitter weather. "Now, should we go and show them how a snowball fight is won?"

"I thought you'd never ask."

With her parents and Em chasing behind, Claire followed Ryan into the cul-de-sac, where the children were hiding behind separate cars. Granny Greta watched on from the window.

Even as a pair of snowballs flew through the sky, both

aiming at Claire like tracked missiles, she knew beyond a doubt that there were no other people in the world with whom she'd rather spend Christmas.

Thank you for reading, and don't forget to
RATE/REVIEW!

The Claire's Candles story continues in...

WILDFLOWER WORRIES
OUT NOW!

WANT TO BE KEPT UP TO DATE WITH AGATHA FROST RELEASES? *SIGN UP THE FREE NEWSLETTER!*

www.AgathaFrost.com

You can also follow **Agatha Frost** across social media. Search 'Agatha Frost' on:

Facebook
Twitter
Goodreads
Instagram

ALSO BY AGATHA FROST

Claire's Candles

1. Vanilla Bean Vengeance

2. Black Cherry Betrayal

3. Coconut Milk Casualty

4. Rose Petal Revenge

5. Fresh Linen Fraud

6. Toffee Apple Torment

7. Candy Cane Conspiracies

Peridale Cafe

1. Pancakes and Corpses

2. Lemonade and Lies

3. Doughnuts and Deception

4. Chocolate Cake and Chaos

5. Shortbread and Sorrow

6. Espresso and Evil

7. Macarons and Mayhem

8. Fruit Cake and Fear

9. Birthday Cake and Bodies

10. Gingerbread and Ghosts

Other

Printed in Great Britain
by Amazon